Arrowsmith

The MacGregors, Volume 1

Elina Emerald

Published by Elina Emerald, 2021.

Table of Contents

Copyright

Dedication

To the survivors and the dreamers...

Chapter 1 – The Past

1036 Edinburgh, Scotland

"I will not leave you, brother, reach for my hand!" Ewan Arrowsmith shouted while desperately trying to help his best friend Robert Wakefield scale the wall. It was too high for Robert's shorter stature, but Ewan now straddled the top, reaching down, trying to pull his best friend over it. From his vantage point, he could see Goldie's men running down the side street, closing the gap between them.

Robert tried several times but stumbled and could not get a foot up.

"No, I cannot reach. You go without me, Ewan, lest Goldie catches you too!" Robert yelled, resigned to his fate. It was his fault they were in this predicament and running for their lives.

Leaving anyone behind was not something Ewan could abide by. He dropped back down from the wall to join Robert on the ground.

"What are ye doing?" Robert shouted in anger. "Get back up there!"

Ewan ignored him, grabbed him around the waist, and physically threw him upward. "Reach!" Ewan shouted.

Robert grabbed the top of the wall and looked over his shoulder at Ewan.

"Get over, Rob! We dinnae have time to waste," Ewan yelled, aware time was running out.

Robert complied and hauled himself up. He then reached down for Ewan.

Ewan backed up a few paces, then ran at the wall, and using the momentum, he took a step and pushed himself upward. He clasped Robert's hand in a firm grip. Then both men scrambled over the wall just as Goldie's men appeared below.

Ewan and Robert landed sure-footed on the other side and sprinted towards the woods.

It was another close call and a lucky escape. Once again, it was Ewan who had saved them both from a disastrous outcome. That was the nature of their unlikely friendship.

Robert was the wealthy heir of a Northumbrian landowner. Ewan was the son of a Scottish farmer from Kinross. Despite the class and demographic divide, they had remained firm friends since meeting at a guild archery tournament in Inverness. Arrowsmith apprenticed in the forge of a nobleman called Macbeth.

Over the years, they had helped each other out of tight binds. But lately, it seemed the older they became, the tighter the binds they found themselves in. After running a distance, they retrieved their horses tethered by a copse of trees and tried to catch their breath. They had managed once more to outrun Goldie and his cutthroat crew. Whether it was adrenaline or humor at the situation, both men burst out laughing with relief at their narrow escape.

"What the hell made you think you could swindle Goldie?" Ewan asked between gulps of air.

"I just figured he would not notice I was cheating." Robert shrugged his shoulders and chuckled.

The two had spent the weekend in Edinburgh drinking and gaming at a local tavern. Both used aliases when they frequented gaming establishments. But this time it almost got them killed. Goldie was a powerful yet unscrupulous proprietor in these parts, and unbeknownst to the two, he owned the tavern Robert tried to swindle. Robert held the winning hand, but he was also cheating, and once discovered, all hell broke loose.

"I've told you plenty of times, Rob, you need to ken your surroundings before you ply your tricks," Arrowsmith grumbled.

"I know, but where's the fun in that?" Rob replied with a cheeky grin.

Once they caught their breath and were sure no one was following them, they set off, this time toward Robert's home.

"You can stay at the estate for a few days and travel home at your leisure," Robert said to Ewan.

Ewan tensed. He did not like that idea. They were not of the same social class. It was one thing to be gaming at taverns together; it was another thing to be sitting at the table of a nobleman. Ewan knew he was not welcome in any of the lavish homes Robert easily gained entrance to because of his birth.

Robert noted Ewan's reluctance and added, "Be at ease, my grandfather has journeyed to Bath. 'Tis only my sister and her chaperone at home. My sister is most likely roaming the countryside gazing at some natural monstrosity."

Ewan relaxed and accepted the invitation. He had been to the Wakefield manor house in the past but never met Robert's family. Ewan's father had warned him not to get too close to peers. But seeing as Robert's estate was closer, he decided it was better to rest there for the night. He could make his way home in the morning.

Once they arrived at the estate, they occupied the east wing and continued drinking and carousing. At least Rob was the one doing the carousing with a pair of giggling maids. Ewan was not in the mood to dally. Being in a large house made him nervous and out of place. After an evening of drunken shenanigans, Ewan was finally shown to a guest bedchamber where a bath was drawn for him. One of the serving women made it clear should he need help with his bath, she was willing. Flattered by the attention, he was uncomfortable taking liberties in his friend's home. Besides, he felt like an impostor and would not take advantage of his host's goodwill.

Arrowsmith turned down her offer, bathed, and slept alone in the largest bed he had ever seen. He decided he would stay an extra day, then hie back to the Highlands. He needed to assist his father with the harvest season and return to Spey Valley in Inverness.

Beth

ELSPETH WAKEFIELD, Beth to her friends, was born into power and privilege. From an early age, it was expected she would marry well and carry on the family tradition of Wakefields marrying into the royal houses of England. Her grandfather and guardian had deigned it to be so ever since Elspeth's mother quit English society and joined a religious order of Beguines. His eccentric son-in-law then had the nerve to die before Beth was nine summers old.

The only problem with that trajectory was that Elspeth inherited her mother's zest for life and her father's disdain for rules. She rarely paid attention to anything her grandfather said. When the strictures of society became too much, she happily lost herself in her paintings, which is why she was up at dawn sitting atop a steep hill sketching subjects from a distance.

Her tutor wanted her to learn Romanesque art designs because iconic figures were all the rage. But Beth preferred real-life subjects to depictions of saints. From her vantage point, she sketched the heart of the estate, everyday yeomen and crofters who worked the land and provided domestic service at the manor. It fascinated her that no one thought to capture their lives in paintings.

Beth loved colors and had an eye for texture and hues. To create something from nothing was the highlight of her day. She began working on the tools of her trade, mixing earthy pigments with egg tempera to create vibrant, bold colors.

Studying her sketches whilst mixing her paints, she was oblivious to the curious feathered creature coveting her tools and waddling closer to her instruments. It wasn't until a long beak plucked the mixing brush from her fingers and took off running that Beth realized she'd been robbed by a goose.

Ewan

IT WAS EARLY IN THE morning as Arrowsmith walked the vast estate. Robert was still abed and most likely would not surface for some time. Arrowsmith was never one to sleep in. Years of helping his father with chores on the farm and training with other men at the forge meant he rose at the crack of dawn, a habit he was apt to maintain. Never one to be idle, Arrowsmith woke early, ate a large breakfast, ignored the maids giving him subtle glances, and ventured outdoors.

He often marveled at the idleness of noblemen. Even if he were a wealthy man, he could never remain idle. He had a strong work ethic and was reliable to a fault.

He was just walking up an incline when he heard a feminine voice cursing and shouting. He also heard intermittent honking sounds. Arrowsmith followed the noise and froze on the spot, not knowing whether to laugh or help because the scene before him was utterly ridiculous.

A young woman in peasant garb was battling a goose that had something in its beak.

"Damn you, give it back, Esmerelda!" she said with one hand around the goose's neck, trying to wrangle it into submission. Her other hand attempted to pry an item out of its beak. The goose swiped her face with its wings in protest. The more the woman yelled, the louder the goose honked.

"Stop it! You know 'tis not polite to steal my things," she hissed.

The recalcitrant goose struggled out of her grip and pecked her on the backside. She yelped; the goose honked. Then it snatched something colorful off her trestle table and ran off with it, its white feathers slowly taking on a cobalt blue tinge. Meanwhile, the woman was covered in red and green hues. She gave chase and caught the recalcitrant goose again. It honked even louder. Turns out it was a call to arms because Arrowsmith witnessed in disbelief several geese warriors cresting the horizon in defense of their kin. A cacophony of nasal monosyllabic honking was their battle cry.

They immediately set upon the young woman and attempted to peck her to death. He was already moving towards her when he heard a muffled voice say, "Oh no, you will not win! You tiresome creatures."

She held steadfast to the item within the assailant's beak before she stumbled and disappeared beneath a flurry of feathers and beaks. Arrowsmith spotted a flash of a shapely thigh and ankles before the gaggle swallowed her up.

Arrowsmith chuckled as he waded into the heart of the feathery war zone. He narrowly escaped several winged attacks as he wrenched out a disheveled, cursing, hissing creature with dark brown curls, covered in blue paint and feathers. She came out the victor because firmly clasped in her hand was the object she had fought so hard to win.

Arrowsmith shooed the gaggle away, and the offending goose, with an indignant glare upon its avian face, honked once more, got one last peck on the woman's bottom before leading its battalion away.

Arrowsmith just stared at her, his eyes shining with restrained laughter. She was a mess.

"That blasted bird thinks she owns the place," she said as she tried to wipe the paint off her dress and her hands. When she finally looked up, Arrowsmith felt like someone had punched him in the gut. He took a sharp intake of breath, and his step faltered because she was a vision. Suddenly he was a shy, untried boy.

"Thank you for coming to my rescue. 'Tis very kind of you." She smiled at him and held her hand out towards him.

Arrowsmith was smitten. He glanced at her hand, then at her, and did not move.

"Well, are you going to shake it or just look at it?" she asked.

Arrowsmith blushed and shook her hand.

"I am Beth. Pleased to meet you."

"I am Ewan, but my friends just call me Arrowsmith."

"Pleased to make your acquaintance, Ewan," she replied, not wanting to presume a friendship so soon. Beth released his hand and returned to her painting tools, trying to clean up the mess the goose had left behind.

"Are you new to the area, Ewan? I have not seen you in these parts."

Arrowsmith loved the way she said his name. "I am just visiting a friend at the manor house," he replied.

"You are friends with Robert Wakefield?" she asked, raising an eyebrow.

"Aye, I am."

Beth stopped to take his full measure. The lilt of his accent was Scottish. She thought his brogue was very charming, and she was trying hard not to blush because he was very handsome. There was a rugged appeal about him. He was a masculine specimen, like a sculpture chiseled from rock. She wished she could sketch his likeness someday. There was a depth of character in his eyes, and his hands showed signs of hard work. Solid hands, solid heart.

They remained silent for some time, both trying to think of something to say, when Arrowsmith's eyes lighted on a sketch sitting on a wooden support made of poplar birch.

The drawing was exquisite. It was just a charcoal sketch, but she had drawn the exact likeness of the gardener. The artistry mesmerized

Arrowsmith. She had captured the very essence of the gardener at work. The details in his hands, the lines in his brow, and the dogged determination on his face as he tilled the soil. Arrowsmith thought her talent extraordinary.

"Oh, that's nothing." Beth blushed and snatched the sketch off the easel and away from his view. "'Tis just a... I'm just trialing some new style of drawing."

"'Tis verra beautiful, lass. You have an exceptional talent to capture his likeness so well."

Beth was embarrassed at his praise. "'Tis not very Romanesque... I should paint more iconic figures."

Arrowsmith replied, "I dinnae ken what any of that means, but you have a gift."

She blushed and started fussing with things on her trestle table.

"I make a terrible artist. My tutor expects me to study more refined figures."

"Pardon my ignorance, but why?"

"'Tis what they expect of painters these days." Beth shrugged her shoulders.

Arrowsmith had nothing much to say to that statement. He was fascinated with the tools of her trade. There were two egg yolks on the table and pigments of different colors.

"What do you use the eggs for?" he asked.

Beth's face lit up. No one ever asked her about her painting technique. It was nice to talk about art for a change. She could not understand why, but she found it easy conversing with Ewan, and she started blathering on.

"I mix the pigments with the egg yolk to create shiny colors for my paintings. The yolk creates a protective barrier so the colors last longer. 'Tis a cheaper method than using oil."

She glanced at Arrowsmith and noticed he was listening to her intently, as if imagining how the process worked. And that was how

Arrowsmith and Beth struck up a friendship, discussing painting techniques.

Eventually, Arrowsmith settled on a tree stump beside her and watched as Beth brought color and vibrant life to the gardener's sketch. Before long, they had fallen into a comfortable conversation about many other topics. Beth became even more animated as she spoke about things she had seen on her travels, and Arrowsmith shared about the tools of his trade as a bowyer at the forge. Beth listened with fascination, wishing she could watch him fashion a bow and arrowhead sometime.

Arrowsmith knew at that moment he had found the woman he wanted to make a life with. His dream had always been a simple one: to earn a good living from his craft, marry a bonnie woman, and create a family and a home for them to live in peace. He decided Beth was that woman, and judging by her clothing and her down-to-earth manner, he reasoned she must be an artist in training of some sort. If he took her with him to Inverness, after they married, of course, she could likely ply some of her trade for noble families.

Arrowsmith was smiling as he gazed at Beth while she talked about a festival she had attended earlier that year. He was already mapping out his life with her when they were interrupted by someone approaching.

"Arrowsmith, there you are! Blast, I have been looking for you everywhere. I see you have met my sister Beth," Robert said whilst on horseback.

Robert burst out laughing at the sight of Beth. "Bug, you look horrendous," he said, calling her by her pet name.

Beth glared at her brother for calling her 'bug' in front of a guest. But it was when she glanced at Arrowsmith that she felt a strange tension.

Arrowsmith stood immediately and stepped away from her. His body stiffened, and his entire demeanor changed. The relaxed, jovial man she had spent the morning conversing with was gone.

Beth felt the weight of his judgment, and she knew not why.

Robert rolled his eyes. "'Tis only Arrowsmith, and I am certain he thinks my sister resembles a bug too."

Arrowsmith's dream shattered with Robert's declaration. She was Robert's sister? Damn him to hell! He knew then she was beyond his reach. His eyes shuttered, and the warmth left them.

"I see," Arrowsmith said and remained quiet. He was a farmer's son and a guild bowyer. She was so far above his station in life there was no point pursuing the acquaintance. What a fool he was.

"Come, let's return to the house. Cook has prepared a lavish feast for us!" Robert said.

Arrowsmith nodded his head. He silently helped Beth pack her things and followed the siblings back to the manor. He refused to make eye contact with her or engage in conversation, such was his disappointment at his future loss.

Chapter 2 – Young Love

Wakefield Manor, Northumbria

During their luncheon, Arrowsmith informed Robert he would take his leave after the noonday meal.

Robert scoffed, "Do not be ridiculous, Arrowsmith. 'Tis too late to set off now. At least stay another night."

"There is to be a storm later. It would be best to remain here and set off on the morrow," Beth said.

"I think 'tis best if I leave today. I have much to attend to in Scotland." Arrowsmith clenched his jaw and averted his eyes. He had mostly ignored Beth throughout the meal.

"No, I insist you stay longer," Robert replied. "One more night will not kill you, Arrowsmith. I also have some fine wine I want to share, so you must stay. I insist upon it." Robert stood and declared he was heading to the cellar for more wine.

Arrowsmith and Beth remained seated on opposite sides of the dining table, alone.

After a few moments of silence, Beth asked, "Have I offended you?"

Arrowsmith glared at her for the first time and bit out, "Why did you not tell me you are Robert's sister and mistress of this house?"

Beth replied, "It did not occur to me to bandy that about when we were talking." She was confused by his reaction.

Arrowsmith snorted. "Right. So, you traipse around in peasant clothing pretending to be an artisan so you can trifle with lowly men like me?"

Beth slammed her fork down on her plate. "I wear old painting smocks, so I do not have to worry about ruining my clothes. And when I met you, I did not care who you were, only that you were polite enough to rescue me from bloody geese!"

Arrowsmith gritted his teeth, and Beth glared back then said, "I do not know why you are angry with me, sir."

Arrowsmith clenched his jaw and said, "Dinnae call me sir. I am a farmer's son. I have no titles."

Beth replied, "Neither do I, Ewan. I am addressed as 'Miss,' and everything I have is tied to an estate I can never inherit. So, if you think I care about titles or that I played you false, then that says more about you than it does about me."

Arrowsmith was taken aback. He had never received a firm dressing down from a lass before. He had to admit Beth was right. At no point had she led him on or pretended to be anything other than who she was. He was being unjustifiably rude, even though she had been nothing but kind and attentive.

"I am sorry, lass. You are right," he replied. "I apologize for my attitude towards you."

Beth nodded, accepting the apology bearing no grudge. "Then you will stay a little longer, I presume?" she asked.

"Aye, a little longer. Someone has to help Robert drink his wine." Arrowsmith grinned.

Beth smiled in return. The tension within the room dissipated as they fell into a comfortable rapport like they had that morning.

When Robert rejoined them with more wine, Arrowsmith was grinning like a fool, and Beth kept casting him subtle glances.

By the time Arrowsmith retired to his bedchamber, he was no longer in danger of falling in love. He was already there.

It was no surprise then that three days later Arrowsmith was still in Northumbria. Robert's grandfather was not due back for several days, so the three friends spent a great deal of time enjoying the warmer weather and the outdoors.

Robert often slept in until midday while Arrowsmith accompanied Beth on her painting expeditions in the early mornings. He loved spending time with her, and they usually took a picnic. On this day, Beth had sketched some ruins. It was a secluded area deep in the woods surrounding the estate, and it was where they shared their first kiss.

Playing with Fire

ARROWSMITH KNEW HE was playing with fire, but he was completely at Beth's mercy. He sought her company every time and was on hand should she need help fighting off the wildlife. She was the first person he thought about when he woke up and the last person when he went to sleep. He dallied longer, stretching out as many days before he needed to return to Moray.

With grey clouds looming, he and Beth set out hoping to capture the sunset over the ruins. They enjoyed a light repast Cook had prepared. Arrowsmith ate alongside her, falling ever deeper into love. When it was just the two of them, there was no class difference even though Arrowsmith was aware of it. Beth treated him like Robert did. In an ideal world, they could be together, but he knew she was off-limits, yet he could not stay away. He gave himself one more day to make memories that would last him a lifetime.

It was midday, and they were lounging on their sides on the rug, propped up with one elbow.

Arrowsmith gazed at Beth then said, "'Tis beautiful out here, lass. 'Tis a pity I canna stay much longer. I must return to my duties."

"Oh?" She looked sad.

"Why the sad face?" Arrowsmith asked.

"'Tis just that I will miss you, Ewan. I have enjoyed your company these past few days."

"I have enjoyed yours too, Beauty."

She stared at him with longing and licked her lips.

Arrowsmith growled. "Dinnae stare at me like that, Beth."

"Like what?" She leaned in closer.

"You need to move away; you are tempting my resolve." He clenched his jaw.

Beth felt relief knowing that this strange attraction she felt for Ewan was mutual.

She whispered, "What if I do not want to move away, Ewan? What if I want you too?"

Arrowsmith closed the distance between them. He leaned forward and before he thought better of it, his lips were on hers.

Beth was startled but did not pull away. Instead, she moved deeper into his embrace.

Arrowsmith could tell she was innocent and untried, and he was undone. He pulled her into his arms and took over the kiss, savoring the sweetness. When he reluctantly pulled away, they were both breathless. No words were necessary between them now, only lingering caresses.

That would be the first of many shared kisses. Over the next two days, their trysts became passionate, but Arrowsmith made sure never to go too far although his control was waning. They snuck kisses in the hallways and alcoves about the house as their budding new romance developed.

Arrowsmith craved more, but he was mindful this was temporary. A farmer's son could never marry a woman of the peerage. He needed to make sure he could cut ties when the time came, with no lasting damage.

After two days of stolen kisses, Arrowsmith knew he could remain no longer. Rather than purge the obsession he had for Beth, it only increased tenfold. He knew she was becoming attached to him as well. He needed to put an end to it. They could never be more than just stolen kisses in hidden places.

Goodbyes

"ROBERT TOLD ME YOU are leaving. Is this true?" Beth asked with tears shimmering in her eyes. She was unsure what to do and felt extremely upset.

"Aye, love, 'tis why I will not take any further liberties with you. You need to reserve such things for the man you marry."

"What if you are the man I wish to marry?" Beth said defiantly.

Arrowsmith clenched his fists to keep himself from reaching for her. He had requested they meet at the ruins so he could explain why he needed to leave and why they could no longer carry on their romance.

"You mean the world to me, Beth, but you and I come from different worlds. I must return to Inverness and my duties to Macbeth, and you have duties to your grandfather and brother. It could never last long between us."

"I see," Beth replied, wearing a mournful expression.

"Dinnae be sad, love. You will ken in time I am doing you a great service. I am not good enough for you."

"No! Do not say those words to me. You are far too good for me, Ewan," Beth replied, as she hugged him for comfort.

Arrowsmith's heart was breaking, but he needed to be stronger for both their sakes. He wrapped his arms around her, resting his chin on the top of her head and said, "I'll miss you, Beth."

"I'll miss you too, Ewan. May I write you sometime?"

"Aye, love, I would like that."

"Then I promise to write often."

They embraced once more for the last time, and Arrowsmith returned to his life in Inverness, determined to put Beth behind him forever. There was no point craving what he could not have, even though he felt a hollow feeling in his chest.

Chapter 3 – The Making of Arrowsmith

1037 – Moray, Scotland

For a year, Arrowsmith threw himself into his work and service. The nobleman Macbeth who he served now ruled the Mormaerdom of Moray, which covered the Spey Valley around Inverness. Macbeth's rise in power elevated anyone in his service.

Arrowsmith heard rumors at the forge that Macbeth was preparing to make a play for the throne of Scotland, so Arrowsmith continued to train with the warriors every chance he got. It was a good way to test whether the weapons he forged worked in battle, and it enabled him to hone his combat skills.

Arrowsmith's work ethic, fighting ability, and quality craftsmanship did not go unnoticed by Macbeth. He used Arrowsmith's skills for his political purposes.

Arrowsmith thought only of bettering his position in society and making good money. But no matter how hard he tried to forget Beth, he could not.

Beth kept to her word and wrote him letters with regularity. He lived for her letters and the emotions they evoked within him. Despite the surrounding temptations from women at the Keep, he never strayed, as Beth's letters kept coming.

She told him of her day and included sketches, so he had a visual representation as well. Arrowsmith treasured these above anything else. He savored every word and every painting. He kept her letters close at night when he slept. Subconsciously, it made him strive harder to make something of himself.

Arrowsmith sent the odd message to Beth when he was not away on a mission. However, by Winter, correspondence was minimal, and by Spring, it ceased altogether.

The cessation coincided with two things. The first was Arrowsmith was now working directly for Macbeth as an informant, so he was away for weeks on end.

By the same token, Beth's letters remained unanswered for so long she deduced that Arrowsmith no longer felt anything for her. That winter, Beth went through a strange mourning period, realizing that her heart was indeed broken, and with no word from Arrowsmith, she put aside her foolish notions of romance and closed that chapter of her life.

It was time to forget Ewan and move on. Her grandfather had been pressuring her to think of marriage. She thought maybe it was time she listened to him for a change.

Meanwhile, Arrowsmith carried her old letters with him wherever he traveled and re-read them repeatedly. The deeper he moved in treacherous and deceitful circles, the more he thought of Beth.

Arrowsmith treasured one miniature painting. It was of two lovers standing within the ruins, locked in an intimate embrace. That became his prized possession. Beth's artwork kept him tethered to a world of truth and goodness when all around him lay treachery and lies.

As the weeks progressed with no more correspondence, Arrowsmith became restless.

Then he received a missive from Robert. It was the usual news of what adventures he was on, but Arrowsmith stilled when Robert imparted that Beth was being pursued by several gentlemen vying for her hand, and he found it bothersome to chaperone her.

Arrowsmith felt a sharp pain in his chest at the news. He screwed up the letter and threw it in the fire, gripped the mantle, and watched the letter burn to ash.

1038 - Berwick upon Tweed, Northumbria

BETH DANCED ANOTHER reel with yet another young man vying for her attention. Lord Lemington was his name. He was wealthy, had Cumbrian connections, and was the dullest man she had ever had the misfortune to meet.

But she pasted a smile on her face and tried to repress a yawn as he outlined his achievements. At no point did he ask questions of her.

"Miss Wakefield, I hope you realize what compliment I pay you by dancing with you right now. Several women have been trying to capture my attention and quite failing."

"Yes, that must be truly tedious," Beth said, stifling a yawn.

"Tedious is an understatement. But I cannot blame them, seeing as I am an accomplished and wealthy gentleman. There are very few men who have achieved what I have. If I were a warrior, I am sure I would be the best the world has ever seen."

Beth raised an eyebrow because she doubted Lemington could wield a sword without stabbing himself. He lacked coordination dancing, which did not bode well if he took to a battlefield.

"Do tell, Lord Lemington, why are you not a warrior now?" Beth asked.

"Mama said 'tis unseemly for a lord to fight his own battles."

They twirled about the room, and Beth thought about his comment then said, "But I have heard that kings fight their own battles. Why would it be different for a lord?" Beth asked. She thought of Ewan. He would have no problem fighting on a battlefield.

Lord Lemington looked as if he had swallowed a lemon.

"You are always so astute, Miss Wakefield. My mama says women should not have opinions on things they do not understand."

"I find it strange then that your mother, who is a woman, has opinions on battles yet she is not a warrior," Beth replied, raising her eyebrow.

Lemington opened his mouth, then closed it again, lost for words.

Fortunately, the dance ended, and Beth excused herself to get some fresh air.

She made her way out the side entrance to a small terrace that overlooked the rose garden. It was a place she and Ewan had sneaked kisses in the past. She touched her lips, remembering what his kiss felt like, and cursed herself for thinking of a man who cared nothing for her.

Beth placed her hands on the iron cast railing and stared up at the night sky, wondering if Ewan was looking up at the same stars. She wondered if he was alone or with another woman when a familiar voice asked, "Did you enjoy your dance, love?"

Beth almost screamed in fright as Arrowsmith stepped out from behind the foliage.

"Ewan! You scared me half to death." She gasped when he gave her a quelling look and pulled her into the shadows. Her back was against the wall as his body caged her in. Their lips were mere inches apart.

"Who was that man you were dancing with?" he growled.

"What on earth are you doing here?"

"I want his name, Beth."

"Lemington."

"What's he to you?"

She was confused and shocked that he was standing so close, that he was even in Northumbria.

"He's nothing, just a man my grandfather wants me to become acquainted with."

"Has he kissed you?"

"No!"

"Has any other man kissed you?"

"Again, no!"

"Good."

"How dare you—" Beth's words were cut off when Arrowsmith's lips came crashing down on hers. He kissed her with a fierceness and a deep longing he had craved for months.

Beth melted into his embrace with abandon.

The kiss turned into gentle nips and bites on her lips.

When Arrowsmith pulled away, he was breathless. "You promised you'd write, Beth, but the letters stopped." He frowned and gently caressed her cheek.

"I did not hear from you, Ewan. I assumed you forgot about me." Beth glanced up at him as his hazel eyes bored deep into her soul.

She turned away, embarrassed when he caught her chin and turned her face towards him.

Arrowsmith had missed her, and she looked ravishing with the gossamer gown and fitted bodice. "I could never forget you, Beth. Your soul is linked to mine."

She snorted. "So, you do not have other women tucked away in Moray?"

"None. Yours are the last lips I have kissed, Beth."

She stared in disbelief.

"If you've come to see Robert—"

"I have not come for Robert. I have come for you, Beth."

"Why?"

"Because you are mine!" Arrowsmith growled.

Before Beth could ponder that statement, she was hoisted over Arrowsmith's shoulder as he swung his legs over the railing and jumped down the short distance to the ground, then stalked away from the party. He knew full well he was risking everything, but he was done playing games. She was the shining light in his dark world, and it was time he claimed what was his.

"Ewan! Put me down!" she hissed.

"When we get to the ruins. I want to spend time with you."

"I cannot, Ewan. If I am discovered—"

"Quiet, Beth, people will hear you." He smacked her bottom.

Beth gritted her teeth and fumed.

Arrowsmith was careful to stay hidden in the shadows.

Several minutes later, she was on his lap atop his horse and riding into the woods.

They had made it to the ruins twenty minutes later in total silence. Beth was still fuming because every time she turned her head to give Arrowsmith a piece of her mind, he kissed her. She was losing her ability for reasoned argument because she enjoyed his kisses and being in his arms again.

Arrowsmith built a small fire, shielded from the wind, and wrapped Beth in his woolen plaid. They huddled together in the same secluded spot where they had shared their first kiss. The sky was filled with stars as they stared up at the heavens.

"Why have you brought me here, Ewan? Why are you here at all?"

"I told myself to let you go, Beth, but after a year, I found I canna do that."

"What are you suggesting?"

Arrowsmith stood and started pacing. "I have amassed a small fortune working for Macbeth. I have a reputable occupation to create more opportunities for myself... for us."

"What do you mean 'us'?"

Arrowsmith stopped pacing and stared at her before he said, "I have means, Beth, to provide for you, if you will have me. I have no title, but I have skills and determination to make a good life for us. I want you close to me always."

"Are you proposing marriage, Ewan?" She looked shocked.

Arrowsmith got down on bended knee before her. "Aye, love, I am. I need you, Beth. I want to raise a family with you, make a life together. I tried to stay away, but the thought of losing you to someone else is unbearable."

There was a long pause as Beth contemplated the proposal.

"I will request permission of your family, of course, but I wanted to hear your acceptance."

Beth was stunned, and her silence was deafening especially to Arrowsmith, who was now regretting his actions in case the woman in question was no longer interested in him.

"I see I have shocked you. I am sorry; I just thought maybe you felt the same way. I must have been wrong—"

"I do!" Beth blurted out, interrupting him.

"You what?"

"I agree to be your wife."

Arrowsmith's entire face lit up, and then he was on her in a flash. She tumbled backward onto the blanket with him above her.

"You do? You speak in truth... you will have me?" he asked, scarcely believing it.

"Yes, with no reservations."

Arrowsmith kissed her then, just as the skies opened up and a storm broke through their joyous reunion.

The Bothy

BETH AND EWAN RAN TO a nearby abandoned cottage so they could wait out the rain.

Safely inside, Ewan found a tinderbox and kindling and started a fire.

"You'll need to take your clothes off, love, before you catch your death. I swear I'll not look."

He turned away as Beth complied.

Arrowsmith could hear the rustling of her gown being removed and tried not to think about the naked body beneath.

"I need your help, Ewan; I cannot untie the back."

Arrowsmith gritted his teeth. He was hard as granite. He clenched his fists but did as she asked. In the fire's light, her pale skin glowed as he removed her surcoat and kirtle. He did not want to think of the fact she was now naked, standing before him and wearing his plaid with his clan colors. A feeling of possessiveness came over him.

He stepped away to remove his clothing.

Several minutes later, their clothes hung beside the fire, drying while they traipsed around in plaid and blankets.

Beth had rummaged for some food. The cottage was well-stocked to cater to these types of weather changes. She prepared a light repast whilst Arrowsmith fetched them water from outside to heat.

They huddled together by the fire for warmth, and Arrowsmith lowered his head and took her lips with his. Beth instigated more and shuffled closer. It broke his resolve. He could no longer fight the attraction; he had to have his woman. He knew then she would be his forever from this moment on. With that in mind, they discarded the covers between them, revealing themselves to one another as he laid her down in front of the fireplace.

On a bed of plaid and blankets, Ewan covered Beth's body with his own and introduced her to the art of lovemaking. From slow embers to a raging inferno, they joined their bodies in a dance as old as time. He moved inside her, and she responded with passion. For the rest of the night, they took their pleasure again and again, learning their way around one another, building their need to match the raging storm outside.

"Ewan!" Beth cried his name as she climaxed.

"Beth!" Arrowsmith shouted as he filled her with his essence. Months of pent-up need finally satisfied and brought to loving completion. They collapsed into each other's arms and slept the satisfied sleep of young love.

By the following morning, Beth was no longer a maiden because Arrowsmith had claimed her and marked her as his. He held her in his arms, knowing that he was one step closer to fulfilling his dream. He had money, and he had means, and beside him in the new light of day, he had a bonnie fiancée.

They stole soft kisses and talked of the future, never realizing their lives were about to change forever because true love rarely runs smoothly the first time around.

Chapter 4 - Discovery

By mid-morning, Beth and Arrowsmith had washed using water he collected and heated, and they were dressing to return to the manor when the door to the cottage burst open.

"What the devil is going on here?" Arthur Wakefield looked irate. "We have been searching all night for you!"

"Grandfather!" Beth gasped.

Arrowsmith pushed her behind him to cover her undressed state. "'Tis not what it looks like," he said.

"Do you think me daft, boy? 'Tis exactly what it looks like!" Arthur lifted his walking stick and struck Arrowsmith across the face. He did not flinch or retaliate; he would not hit an old man.

Beth screamed and tried to get around Ewan, but he kept her behind him.

"How dare you put your vile hands on her," Arthur seethed. "She's made for royalty, and now you have sullied her with your baseborn prick!"

Arrowsmith clenched his fists but still did not move.

"Grandfather, stop!" Beth gasped in outrage at his vicious words.

"Don't 'grandfather' me, you trollop! You have ruined yourself," Arthur spat.

Ewan said, "I intend to marry her."

"I should hope not!" Arthur replied, an appalled expression on his face.

"Grandfather, they should marry in haste." Robert now entered the cottage and closed the door as servants and serfs milled about the lane. No doubt word had spread about their mistress's disappearance.

"You stay out of this, Robert. Need I remind you about your minor problem?" Arthur seethed.

Robert blushed bright red.

Beth wondered what problem he referred to.

"My intentions towards Beth are honorable. I will marry her and provide for her," Arrowsmith repeated, now clutching Beth's hand in his. "I love your granddaughter, and I will care for her until my dying breath."

Beth gazed at him. Arrowsmith gave her a meaningful glance and squeezed her hand. He was genuine. A powerful surge of emotion passed between them, and Beth returned a soft smile.

Their intimate moment was ruined when Arthur said, "You will do no such thing. This is outrageous. Your path is mapped out, Beth." He pointed his finger at her. "You will marry this man over my dead body. If I had known the scandal you would create cavorting with this heathen, I would have drowned you at birth."

Arrowsmith felt affronted. "I can provide for Beth. I have excellent prospects—"

"You have no title, or fortune, or family seat. Therefore, you have nothing!"

"'Tis not true, Grandfather. Ewan works for a nobleman. He has a grand future ahead of him."

"He is a lowly Scot. His reputation is dirt around here. Robert, get this garbage off my land and take your sister back to the house, or I will call the Shire Reeve." Arthur stormed away without another word. He could be heard snarling at servants, telling them to go home. They immediately averted their eyes and moved away.

Robert was quiet for a moment, as if torn between family duty and his best friend. He hesitated for several moments as Arrowsmith just glared at him and Beth looked defiant.

"Ewan, you're my closest friend, but you have nothing to offer her."

Arrowsmith was furious because there it was. Even his best friend thought him incapable of providing for her.

Then Robert continued, "You are my best friend, and I know you are an honorable man. But if you could make something of yourself, to prove to our grandfather that you can provide for Beth, it might make things easier."

Robert was letting them know he was on their side.

Arrowsmith felt guilty that he had not been more open with him. "'Tis sorry I am, brother, you must find out about us like this. I owed you greater courtesy."

"I suspected you had formed an attachment to Bug. I just had far greater..." He hesitated. "More pressing matters to contend with. I approve of your union, but I do not hold the purse strings. 'Tis my grandfather you must convince."

Beth, who was now fully dressed, launched herself at her brother and hugged him. "Truly you approve?"

"I only want to see you happy, Bug, but you know how grandpa is, he hates being taken by surprise."

"Then how do you suggest we proceed?" Arrowsmith asked.

"Prove to him you have means to provide for Beth that will be advantageous to him. My grandfather is an ambitious man."

Arrowsmith knew there was something he could do. But he would have to run it by Macbeth first, which meant he would need to leave Beth for a short period and return with an offer her grandfather could not refuse.

BEFORE TAKING HIS LEAVE, Arrowsmith struck a deal with Robert.

"Robert, I ask you this as someone who always had your back. I now ask you to have mine."

"Go on."

"Brother, I am trusting you to take care of Beth. Prevent your grandfather doing anything hasty, no marrying her off to some beau. I have a plan, and I will return soon."

"All right, I will appease the old man until your return. Whatever you have planned, Ewan, make it worth it."

"You can count on it."

Don't Go

ARROWSMITH TOOK HIS leave of Beth and shared his plans.

"Macbeth has requested I join an elite force loyal to him. I have been putting it off, but he offered me anything I want should I accept. I will request some land where we can make a home, and in time I can work my way up to a loyal thane or vassal."

Beth was not having a bar of it.

"Ewan, I do not need those things. We can run away together now. We can elope and just marry. Come, let's go right now." Beth was desperate; she had a foreboding feeling.

"I canna do that to you, Beth. Robert is right. You need your grandda's approval. Besides, where will we live? In the forge?"

"Why not? I can be happy anywhere as long as you are there."

"No, Beth, you need finer things. I should not have offered for you without a solid plan, and I ken a way to do it. But I must return to Inverness first and plan, then I will return for you in a fortnight."

"I do not want to wait, Ewan, please... I have a bad feeling about this. Take me with you. I am old enough to know my mind. I love you; I have given myself to you. Please, let's just run away together." She pleaded and gripped his arm, trying to make him see reason.

"No, love, it will bring scandal to your name. Trust me, wait for me and ken I will return for you, Beth, I promise."

Resigned to her fate, she said, "Then I will wait for you, Ewan. No matter how long it takes, I will wait for you. But please wear this for protection." She handed over a silver cross-chain and placed it around his neck.

"No, Beth, I canna take this. 'Tis too precious."

"Then return it to me when I see you again."

"I love you, Beth. Never doubt it. We will be together forever. What are a few more days of waiting? I need you to trust me, trust us," Arrowsmith pleaded.

"I love you, Ewan, and I trust you. I will wait for you," Beth said with tears shimmering in her eyes. She hugged him, and they shared an intimate embrace.

If only she had known that would be the last kiss they would share, she would have made it last longer. And if Arrowsmith knew what lay ahead, he would have eloped that day.

THE MOMENT ARROWSMITH left, Rob looked over the parchment his grandfather had already signed. There was a blank space for his signature. It was a contract from Earl Siward of Northumbria. The offer was too valuable to reject.

His overwhelming debts paid in exchange for Beth.

He hesitated but a second, then signed Beth's life away.

Robert then whispered, "Forgive me, Arrowsmith, but sometimes we cannot have what we want."

Macbeth's Man

A SENNIGHT LATER, ARROWSMITH finally accepted his place as part of an elite group of men who worked in service to Macbeth. His role was to immerse himself even deeper in treachery and deceit as he spied on several key figures in different parts of Scotland. In exchange for his service, he received a parcel of land and an annuity to provide for his new wife.

Arrowsmith had one last mission to attend to, then he could return to Beth.

Under the cover of darkness, Arrowsmith balanced on a tree branch high above the ground. He was in Culbin Forest, just outside of Moray. Two arrows were nocked against the tight bowstring as he waited for his target. He wore a hooded black cloak and blended in with the shadows.

After an hour, a man stepped into the clearing. He held a missive.

"Got you!" Arrowsmith whispered to himself. It was his target. He aimed and fired. His arrows struck true as his target crumpled to the ground.

Arrowsmith descended and leaped the final meter to the ground. He made his way to his target, bent down, and pocketed the missive, then dragged his body into thickets nearby. His task complete, Arrowsmith was elated; he could finally return to Northumbria. He quickly made his way back to the forge with Macbeth's stolen parchments, documents that would never get into enemy hands now.

That night, Arrowsmith celebrated at the local tavern with some other guild apprentices who heard he was soon to be married. He was careful not to over-imbibe as he had a long journey to make in the morning. Full of hope and excitement to see Beth, he excused himself early to walk back to the Keep alone. Distracted with thoughts of Beth, he did not see the attack coming until it was too late. A blow to the back of the head. He staggered forward when a hand ripped the necklace from his neck before everything went black.

Chapter 5 – Tragedy

The Quickening

Beth patiently waited for word from Ewan as two weeks became three, then six, and still no word arrived. Under any other circumstances, she would have waited forever, but the problem was her courses were late, and Beth knew she was slowly increasing with Ewan's babe. It was becoming noticeable even to Robert that her bouts of nausea only occurred in the mornings.

Robert said he would look after her. She trusted he would shelter her long enough until Ewan returned. She never doubted that Ewan would return to her soon.

"Bug, because you are enceinte, you will remain here until I can make plans," Robert said.

Beth asked, "Then you will find Ewan and get word to him I am with child?"

"Of course, I will, Bug. Your child needs his father," he replied.

BY THE FOLLOWING MONTH, a parchment arrived for Beth. Robert read it to her. It was from Inverness. It was brief and to the point: Ewan Arrowsmith was dead. Inside the package was a silver cross-chain necklace.

Beth clutched it to her breast and collapsed onto the floor, sobbing inconsolably. She wept for several days, her heart irrevocably broken. The only thing keeping her alive was the babe growing in her womb, the one reminder of the greatest love she had ever known. She would do everything in her power to make sure the child grew strong, and someday she would speak of its father, a man who stole her heart.

That week, Robert broached the subject of marriage with her again. "Bug, you must marry soon, before you show even more. You cannot live with the scandal. I have arranged someone for you; he is wealthy and with means. His name is James Davenport, and he is from Bamburgh."

"I will not marry him under false pretenses. He needs to know I carry another man's child, or I will not marry him."

"He already knows; 'tis a delicate issue."

"What do you mean?" she asked.

"James needs an heir, but he cannot sire one. 'Tis why he has agreed. No one else will know except for us and Earl Siward."

"What does this have to do with Siward?"

"'Tis none of your concern, Bug; only know this works best for all of us."

Beth nodded and stared out the window of her solar, caressing her belly and knowing the best chance she had of shielding her child from scandal was to indeed marry a stranger. That day she made it her mission in life to protect her babe above all else. First, she would survive. Eat better, build her strength. This was how she could honor Ewan's memory, by protecting their child above all else. If she had to walk through fire, she would.

Little did Beth know that is exactly what she would have to do.

Shattered Dreams

AFTER A WHIRLWIND COURTSHIP, Beth married one James Davenport. He was a dashing nobleman with close ties to Siward, the Earl of Northumbria. A first-class charmer. Pious with high morals, kind, and attentive to her needs. For a grief-stricken woman in desperate need of comfort, he provided a gentle presence with honeyed words. James made her feel cherished, and to Beth's detriment, she fell for every single lie.

Before the ink was dry on their marriage certificate, James's true character emerged. It was anything but pious or gentle. She noticed the first inkling that something was wrong in the first week of their marriage. First, James made it clear they would maintain separate chambers and there was no need to consummate the marriage, seeing as she was already with child.

That suited Beth fine, but it never occurred to her that James would seek his pleasure openly by bringing courtesans into their home for the world to see. Or that Beth would be relegated to a mere visitor while various women occupied his bedchamber.

However, Beth bore it with fortitude and turned a blind eye to scantily clad women walking the hallways at night. But she drew the line with his salacious parties. It was on one such evening that she spoke up and voiced her disapproval. It was the first and last time she ever spoke up again.

House Party

"JAMES, WHO ARE ALL these people?" Beth asked as the house party was in full swing.

"My friends. We will use the North wing tonight, so make yourself scarce."

"What will you all be doing?"

James glared at her as his guests snickered. "What we do is not your concern. Mind your matters, Beth."

"I just wanted to—"

Without warning, James struck her across the face. She stared, stunned, and held her cheek in pain.

"Now look what ye made me do. If you had not questioned me, I wouldn't need to do that," James snapped at her as if it was her fault he struck her.

One woman started laughing and said, "Cor, James, this missus of yours isn't too bright, is she?"

Beth blushed with embarrassment as the men snickered at her predicament, then disappeared down the hall.

James pointed his index finger in her face and said, "If you ever question me in front of my guests again, I will not be held responsible for my actions." He seethed. "Now go to your room and stay there. I do not want to see you again till morning!"

With those parting words, he stormed down the hall with an entourage of guests in tow.

Beth stared after them and retired to her room. Dejected, hurt, and reeling from the incident, she paced her room, thinking of ways she could get out of the marriage.

An hour later, her curiosity was piqued, wondering what they were doing in the North wing, so she slowly stalked to that section of the large manor. The doors were closed, but she could smell opium, and she could hear loud moaning noises coming from behind the door. She took a peek inside, and her blood ran cold. Several guests were naked and openly fornicating within. Some women were coupled with two men, some men with two women, and amidst it all lay her husband, engaging in a public orgy.

Beth gasped in outrage and disbelief. She could not bring up Ewan's child in this environment.

She grabbed one of the crossed swords hanging in the hallway and stormed into the room, waving the sword around. "Get out! How dare you bring debauchery into this house?" she screamed, taking swipes at people.

Women shrieked, men shouted in surprise, trying to avoid the blade.

The last thing Beth saw was an enraged James, naked and striding across the room towards her before his fist connected with her temple.

When Beth came to, she was in her bed, and James was hovering above her. He did not apologize, only reprimanded her further.

"I received many coins to keep you, so you will play the role of dutiful wife and never attack my guests. Do you hear me?"

Beth nodded, too frightened to provoke his volatile temper further.

He was so angry there was spittle coming from his mouth as he spoke. "Your only purpose here is to birth that bloody bastard so I have an heir. If you were not pregnant, I would have thrashed you black and blue, but I need that child to survive. Now mind your own matters, or I will make sure every day you live under this roof will be miserable."

Beth nodded and turned away. She needed to be smart; she was increasing and did not want Ewan's child harmed. She resolved that whatever the future held, she would survive and keep their child safe. He was all she had left in the world. She wished again that Ewan had survived to claim her. Once James left her room, she wept bitter tears of loss and regret.

Endings

EWAN AWOKE FROM HIS attack in different surroundings. He felt his neck and realized the necklace was missing. He tried to sit up, but nausea assailed him, and he collapsed back down. He was disoriented, but all he wanted was Beth.

"Calm yourself; you are safe." He heard a woman's voice. The clan healer. She filled him in on what had happened. He was found by one of Macbeth's guardsmen and delivered to the cottage. They deemed it a common robbery, most likely for his possessions.

Arrowsmith was desperate to leave. It was taking too long to heal, but he had no energy left. The blow to the head had weakened him. He was not strong enough to travel, and he slipped in and out of consciousness. When he was lucid enough, he sent correspondence to Robert that he had suffered a setback but would be there for Beth. But he received nothing in return.

Out of worry and a sense of urgency, he made the journey to Northumbria as soon as he was well enough, which meant by then several weeks had passed. But when he arrived at Wakefield estate, the family was not in. He asked the housekeeper, who informed him, "The Family have quit the countryside and returned to town."

"What about Miss Beth... I mean Miss Wakefield?" he asked.

"Oh, Miss Elspeth is married. She accepted the hand of a nobleman."

He faltered. "Are you sure aboot that?"

"'Tis true. Some fancy gentleman arrived to court her. Head over heels they were." The housekeeper prattled on.

"Is there... is there a message for me at all? My name is Arrowsmith."

"Oh yes, wait here a moment. Master Robert left a note for you should you ever return."

She returned and handed it to him. Arrowsmith thanked her for it and walked back down the footpath. His hands were trembling as he opened it.

It was Robert's handwriting. But when Arrowsmith read the contents, he roared with anger. Beth had left without a word. She had fallen in love with a nobleman.

Robert's note expressed apologies for any hurt feelings, but he stated it was all for the best. Beth was happy, and he urged Arrowsmith to move on with his life.

Arrowsmith felt wretched. Beth had promised to wait forever, yet she could not wait an extra month. A man with a title had replaced him. She told him she cared not about titles, yet deep down inside she must have. A million thoughts went through his head, none of them good.

Arrowsmith vowed right there and then that he would make something of himself. He would be ten times the man this nobleman was, and Beth would regret the loss of him.

Having no reason to mistrust Robert, Arrowsmith accepted the contents of the letter, never thinking to go after Beth. He felt rejected because of his lowly birth; that insecurity plagued him still. Had he been thinking clearly, he might have made a different decision. It was a crucial error that would set them both on a collision course with tragedy.

Arrowsmith returned to Inverness, a crestfallen man. But he was determined to clear his mind of Beth forever.

Chapter 6 – Present Day

1046 Bamburgh Northumbria – *The King's Man in the North*

Arrowsmith splashed cold water on his face, then stared at himself in the reflection glass. He took a long, hard look at the man he had become. He was now the King's Man in the North, ever since Macbeth became King of Scotland. Arrowsmith's importance in the world rose exponentially now that he worked directly for the king. Being a loyal vassal brought him a good level of wealth, respect, power, and privilege. Arrowsmith took care of his parents in their dotage and paid workers to farm the land so his father could live a life of comfort. Not bad for a boy from Kinross who did not even have two sceats to rub together.

He had amassed more wealth than most noblemen, and he managed his estate and investments wisely. Although Arrowsmith also had his pick of women at Court, he'd had very few lovers. None of whom ever measured up to his first love, Beth, and so were destined to fail. The last wound up being a disastrous misjudgment on his part when he invited a spy into his bed.

As Arrowsmith reflected on his life thus far, he realized none of it gave him peace. He was restless all the time. The only solace he had known was when Beth was his all those years ago and again when he met her recently at the safe house at the Cove. Just being in her presence calmed him. But now he was making a bloody mess of things.

If only he had the same effect on her. Beth was skittish around him and avoided him like the plague. She also used Jordie as a shield to prevent any contact between them. Arrowsmith was beyond frustrated, but he knew he needed to take things slow. Still, it hurt to know Beth was avoiding him again. He knew there were years of work ahead, but trying to get any positive reaction out of her was like trying to shuck an oyster with fingernails.

Arrowsmith loved spending time with his son and tried to get Beth to join them, but she made up ridiculous excuses to be somewhere else. He wanted so much to talk to her like they did when they were younger. He wanted to know everything about her. Did she still paint? Whatever happened to Esmeralda the goose? Instead, he had to rely on the meager crumbs of information he could extract from Jordie.

He rubbed his hand over his beard when he thought about Jordan. Arrowsmith smiled at the thought of his son, who inherited his hazel eyes. He could scarce believe it. Jordie was his son. Their son. The woman he loved had given him a bairn, and he did not know until recently. Had it not been for his work with Dalziel Robertson, Beth and Jordie might have been lost to him forever.

Beth named his son Jordan, which was Arrowsmith's middle name. It was his father's middle name and his grandfather's middle name. Beth thought him dead, so she kept his memory alive for their son. That gave him hope. A fierce possessiveness came over him when he thought about his family. Nothing and no one would ever hurt or separate them again.

Arrowsmith recalled the moment he saw Beth at the safe house, that instant moment of recognition when he saw her as his beloved Beth. But there was now a fragility about her that was never there before. She was a timid swan when she used to be a falcon. He knew he had to tread cautiously. He went about doing everything to set up a future home for them all. He lived a celibate life now, and no other woman factored into the equation. He wanted only Beth with a burning desire he could not quench.

It was not lost on Arrowsmith the type of man James Davenport was. He kicked himself that he never thought to dig deeper and find out exactly who Elspeth Davenport was. Arrowsmith dried his face and gritted his teeth. He tried to proceed with caution, but he was done giving her space to decide their future. Jordie needed a father, Beth needed his protection, and Arrowsmith needed his family with him under his roof. His dream had never died: Beth by his side in a house filled with their bairns and love and laughter.

Dalziel told him all that he kenned about Beth's life under her late husband's rule. Arrowsmith felt violently ill at the reports he received. But mostly about the loneliness and isolation she must have felt all these years, having no one else to turn to. He knew she and James had led separate lives and about the sacrifices she had made protecting their son. That Davenport had put his hands on Beth in violence caused him the greatest amount of pain and regret. It was something he could not stomach.

Arrowsmith gripped the water pitcher so hard when he thought of the hell Beth must have gone through, it shattered in his hand. The sharp edges cut into his palm, and he did not feel it.

"Sir, you have cut yourself," his chamberlain said while laying out his clothes for him.

"Aye, so I have."

Arrowsmith's palm was dripping blood. He rummaged through a cabinet for a salve and administered his treatment, then bandaged it. He had done this often enough over the years, tending to his cuts and bruises. Such was the life of the king's man.

"Where are ye off to, sir?" his chamberlain asked.

"I'll be at the Cove if any message comes from Macbeth. Send it there."

"Of course."

Beth

BETH WAS STILL REELING from the knowledge that Ewan was alive, and yet he had never sought her out in seven years. He never searched for her. She maintained her distance, keeping their meetings short and formal. Ewan spent more time with Jordie, which she did not begrudge. She did not even know how to broach the topic of telling Jordie that Ewan was his real father, so she preferred to bury her head in the sand and ignore most things.

She was working at the Cove, where she now helped manage the safe house for Clarissa Robertson. Beth was currently going over the accounts when Arrowsmith appeared in the doorway. It seemed whenever she thought about him, there he was.

"Hello, love," he said.

"He... hello, Ewan," she stammered.

She was nervous, with butterflies in her stomach, and tried to calm her riotous emotions as she took her fill of Ewan. He was breathtaking. He had matured into a man with hard edges and grooves in his eyes. Age and wisdom lent a rugged type of masculinity to his features and a depth of wisdom in his eyes. She saw the boy in him still, but now the grown man was far more prominent in his physique. He was fit and trim and even more handsome than she had ever imagined. He was truly beautiful, and she felt so beneath him.

She cursed her late husband and his mistreatment of her. Her body was scarred, her emotions frayed, and she felt damaged... lesser somehow. For seven years, she had mourned Ewan, and yet there he was standing before her. Time had been kind to him while she felt ravaged by its passing.

"Beth, we need to talk. There is much we need to resolve between us," he said.

She took a deep breath, then replied, "Of course, come in, take a seat. Would you like some tea?"

He shook his head.

Arrowsmith said, "I need to ken what happened that led you to believe I was dead."

"'Tis the past, Ewan. I do not wish to relive one of the most painful memories of my life."

"Please, sweeting, I need to ken what happened. Give me something so I ken how to proceed."

Beth saw the earnestness in his eyes and relented.

"After you left for Inverness, I discovered I was carrying Jordan. I waited, and you did not return or send word as the weeks passed."

"I sent word, Beth, to Robert."

"All I know is a missive arrived several weeks later that you had died."

"What? But I was very much alive. I sent several letters to Robert informing him that I would come for you."

Beth looked confused.

"I was attacked outside the local tavern and robbed, the night before I was to return to you."

She had a horrified expression.

"It took me over a month to recover, but as soon as I was able, I rode straight to you, but you were gone."

"I received no letter, Ewan. After I found out you were dead, I had no choice but to seek marriage. I was increasing with Jordie, and Robert told me I had to protect Jordie's reputation."

"I came for you, Beth, but you did not wait as you had promised."

She flinched. "I thought you were dead, Ewan. Robert even gave me the necklace to prove it."

Arrowsmith stilled and asked, "What necklace?"

Beth uncovered the neckline of her gown and showed him the silver cross she wore daily.

"But how? The thieves, they stole that from me," Arrowsmith replied.

"Robert read out the missive, and this was enclosed in it. When I saw the cross, it was proof you were gone. I knew from your letters that you never took it off. If I had any hope you were alive, I would have waited still."

They were silent a while as they came to the same conclusion.

"Dear Lord, it was Robert," Beth rasped.

"Aye, Robert betrayed us both." Arrowsmith clenched his jaw and fists.

Beth stood and looked at him with such anguish in her eyes. It broke Arrowsmith's heart.

"But why? Why would he do that? To us, Ewan? His best friend and his sister? Seven years, Ewan... seven years he took from us." She brought her hands to her face and burst into tears with deep, heartfelt sobs.

Arrowsmith crossed the distance between them and pulled her into his arms. She buried her face in his chest, clung to him, and wept.

"Shh, sweeting, tis all right now. I will make it all right."

Beth just clung to him tighter. All the regrets, the lost years, because of her brother.

Arrowsmith comforted her. "Where is Robert now?" he asked.

She lay her head on his chest, her arms wrapped around his middle. "We lost touch after I married James. Robert sent me like a lamb to the slaughter and then abandoned me to my hell."

"Whatever the reason, Beth, we have been given a second chance."

She shook her head and pulled away. "We cannot, Ewan. I am not... I am not who I once was." The tears fell as she tried to hold them back.

Arrowsmith pulled her back into his arms. "Shh, love, we'll take it slow. One day at a time."

He tilted her chin up so she was staring at him. Her eyes were bright with emotion. It was too much for him to bear. With a desperate need to comfort her, Ewan bent his head and, before he thought better of it, he kissed her.

For the first time in over seven years, he kissed Beth. Closing his eyes, he savored the feel of her soft lips on his. It was pure, sweet, and all Beth.

Beth was lost in the feeling of something familiar. Deep down, she wanted this connection again. So she stopped resisting and returned the kiss, her arms winding about Ewan's neck as he pulled her into his embrace.

He craved more as he moved in closer, a low groan leaving his lips. He wanted nothing more than to make love to her and move inside her. She was his peace, his solace. He knew Beth was not unaffected because she returned his kiss with fervor and a deep wanting. Her breathing was shallow, and she moaned in response.

"Let go of my mama!" a young voice yelled from behind.

Ewan felt a light hit to his back.

Beth broke off the kiss and blushed deeply, as if startled back to her senses.

Arrowsmith reluctantly let her go and spun around to see Jordie's fist raised, about to punch him in the groin.

"Jordie, no, he was not hurting me." Beth moved around to Arrowsmith's side, trying to placate her furious son.

Arrowsmith dodged the punch, but Jordie managed a swift kick to his shin, giving him the evil eye.

"Jordie! Stop."

Jordie glared up at Ewan, his fists clenched.

"Tis true, Jordan. I was not hurting your ma," Ewan said.

Beth moved forward and pulled Jordie beside her. It was a protective instinct honed through years of living with James. Beth knew Ewan would not hurt Jordie, but survival instincts learned because of abuse were difficult to change.

Ewan noticed the move and frowned. He would cut out his own heart before he hurt either of them. But he let it slide. Given Beth's history, he understood her fear for their son. Not for the first time did he wish he could gut Davenport for the damage he had done.

Ewan gentled his voice and raised his hands, palms up. "I swear to you, I would never hurt your ma."

Jordie scowled at Arrowsmith, then moved forward and tried to push him away. It was futile, as Jordie soon learned when the force of his own pressure coming up against an immovable object caused him to stumble backward. Ewan caught him and helped him regain his footing.

Jordie was embarrassed. He shook off Arrowsmith's arm and glowered.

"I promise all I wanted was your ma to ken how I feel about her," Arrowsmith said, his piercing gaze now on Beth.

"Aye, Jordie, Mr. Arrowsmith and I were just talking," Beth added.

"It did not look like talking. You were attacking my ma with your mouth!" Jordie was outraged, and it took every bit of energy for Arrowsmith to keep a straight face and not laugh.

He heard Beth stifle a giggle.

"And you were very brave to protect her. You have a good swing, son. You'll make a fine warrior someday," Arrowsmith said, now folding his arms across his chest and standing with his legs apart, appraising Jordie.

Jordie puffed up his chest in pride and seemed undecided whether to accept the praise or remain hostile. He chose the former.

"A man has to protect his womenfolk," he said, then mimicked Arrowsmith's stance.

Beth bit her lip to hide her mirth. Jordie was Ewan's son, right down to the marrow.

Arrowsmith's eyes crinkled at the sides as if he wanted to chuckle but he responded in seriousness. "Aye, I can see you have honor. Your ma is verra lucky to have a warrior protecting her... mouth."

Beth just grinned at their inside joke, and Arrowsmith felt as if the sun came out.

He stretched out his arm, offering one hand to Jordie for a handshake.

Jordie puffed up with pride even more and shook Arrowsmith's hand.

"Well, I suppose now that you're here, your ma is in safe hands... but may I give you some fighting tips?"

Jordie sized him up for a moment, then reluctantly nodded.

Arrowsmith crouched down to Jordie's eye level. "Tis best to weigh up the size and strength of your enemy before you take the first swing. Dinnae let emotion or anger drive your actions."

Jordie was quiet and contemplative.

Arrowsmith continued, "A good warrior is not just strong here"—he flexed his arm and tapped his muscle—"but also here." He tapped the side of his head. "Strength and wisdom combined will make you a great warrior someday. You ken?"

Jordie thought on it for a while, then nodded.

"Mayhap you can begin training with me?" Ewan asked as he stood.

Jordie's entire face lit up with excitement, forgetting his earlier anger. "Really?"

"Aye. We can start on the morrow if tis all right with your ma?"

Beth observed how much Jordie loved Ewan's praise and comments. She realized he needed a man in his life to show him how to be a good man. He needed Ewan.

Jordie turned to Beth in eagerness. "Can I, Ma?"

She nodded, knowing that it was probably best her son learned to protect himself better. And there was no one better to teach him than his own father.

"Yes, tomorrow would be a good time. I have to see my solicitor in the morning. It will give you both time to train together."

"Then tomorrow it is, son," Arrowsmith replied, smiling down at Jordie. "I'll take my leave now, but Beth, we're not done. Far from it." Arrowsmith gave her a meaningful glance before he excused himself and left the house.

Nothing

"WHAT DO YOU MEAN JAMES has nothing?" Beth asked her solicitor the following morning.

"Unfortunately, Mrs. Davenport—"

"Tis just Miss Wakefield now. Please address me as such, or just call me Beth. We go back a long way, Carrington; there's no need to stand on ceremony."

Carrington was a handsome Welshman and one of the few men who often helped Beth against Davenport's wishes. It was his contacts who took her in before she sought the help of the safe house refuge owner, Clarissa Robertson.

Carrington also helped other women from the safe house with free legal advice, and he was one of the few men Beth trusted with Jordie's inheritance.

"Very well, Beth, tis sorry I am to say this. James owed vast sums to creditors who have petitioned the Chancellor for payments. The estate is mired in debt."

"But that cannot be. He left a Will with Jordie's entitlements."

Carrington shook his head. "Unless his debts are cleared, the bulk of his estate reverts to the Crown."

Beth slumped into the chair in disbelief. "What am I supposed to do, Carrington?"

"'Tis my advice to sell as many assets as possible to pay down the debt."

Beth nodded, then asked, "How about the house? Can we sell it to recoup funds?"

"No, they tied it up in a complicated trust which could still be untenable if the debts on the main estate are not paid. The good news is you can remain living there; the bad news is it is costly to maintain."

"Can it be leased?"

"That is a possibility."

"At least that's something. What of Jordie? He is Davenport's only heir. What of the coin he was to inherit?"

Carrington looked increasingly uncomfortable.

"What is that look, Carrington? Please, I need the truth."

Carrington cleared his throat and said, "Your late husband left a substantial amount of coin... but he distributed it to a mistress in Anglia who has since disappeared."

"Of course he did," Beth said sarcastically and clenched her fists. Even from the grave, James continued to be a mean-spirited son of a cur.

"I am sorry, Beth, that it has left you in this predicament. I can arrange a discreet auction at your home if that would help ease some of the—"

"Humiliation?"

He nodded.

"Trust me, Carrington, I have survived far worse than mere humiliation. Do whatever you can."

Beth left the solicitor's office feeling despondent. Trust James to leave her and Jordie destitute.

She touched her lips, remembering Arrowsmith's kiss from the day before. It was yet another reason she needed to avoid him. She was damaged goods, and now she was poor-as-a-church-mouse damaged goods. Beth shook her head. No, Ewan was too good for her. He deserved an unscarred beauty without the tarnished past she had just survived. As Beth walked to her next appointment, she felt a tear slide down her cheek, a subconscious reaction to the welling sadness resulting from a profound sense of despair.

Chapter 7 – Pressure

Bamburgh, Northumbria

A month later, it was time for Sale Day. The patrons and interested buyers were due in a few hours, and Jordie was to spend the day with Arrowsmith.

Beth was glad of it; she did not want Jordie around for this spectacle as strangers, valuers, and auctioneers picked through their household items. She trusted Arrowsmith with Jordie, but she did not trust herself. The feelings towards her first love were growing stronger by the day. But Beth still struggled with insecurities and self-doubt. Every time she saw Arrowsmith, it reminded her of the painful past of losing him. If she had to go through that again, she was not sure she would survive it.

Living with James fractured her emotionally. Though her physical wounds healed, inside she was fragile. Spending time with Clarissa Robertson and the MacGregor women had taught her she was not defenseless. She could protect herself. But she had yet to learn how to protect her heart.

If Arrowsmith grew tired of her, or if he kept lovers as James did, that would break her heart just as easily. She heard a little about his relations with other women. It hurt to think of him being intimate with anyone else whilst she spent years alone with only memories. James and his friends gave her a wide berth, and she was glad of it. But it made for a very lonely existence. She promised she would never marry again, and she would keep that promise.

"Mama! Mr. Arrowsmith is here," Jordie shouted while running into her drawing room.

She stood abruptly to greet Arrowsmith as he filled the doorway. He wore trews and coat, looking every bit the gentrified man. She had done some digging, and Arrowsmith was indeed a very wealthy man of means now. He rubbed shoulders with royalty. Beth felt the social gap between them widen. Their meetings were always awkward.

"Mama, Mr. Arrowsmith, he is going to teach me to ride a horse."

Beth looked worried.

"Steady, son, lest your mother has a heart attack. We'll take it slow, Beth, and he'll be safe with me," Arrowsmith said.

"Aye, Mama, Mr. Arrowsmith says we can't shoot arrows from atop the horse until I get better at riding."

Beth paled. "Arrows? From a horse?"

"Och, Jordie, you were not supposed to tell her that." Arrowsmith shook his head and chuckled.

Beth was concerned. "Ewan, he does not know how to ride. He needs—"

"He needs to learn, and I will teach him."

Beth stared at Jordie, who was eager, and she relented. "You are right, Ewan, but please be safe."

Arrowsmith leaned in towards her and whispered in her ear, "I will protect our son with my life, Beth."

He kissed her on the cheek and winked, then led Jordie away.

"I will see you both when you are finished," Beth replied, trying to catch her breath at the intimate gesture.

She knew Ewan was playing a slow game of seduction with her. Subtle touches and caresses, pecks on the cheek. And damn him, it was working. Beth shook her head. She needed to focus. She was glad he was not around for the auction. She had not told him of her predicament; it just was none of his business. As long as he was occupied with Jordie, all would be well.

Warrior in the Making – Bamburgh Cove

ARROWSMITH RAN THROUGH the woods surrounding the Cove. He remained hidden but kept pace from a distance. Several yards away, Jordie ran, paused for a moment to nock his arrow, then fired at the round target which was moving. The shot went wide. Jordie sprinted and picked up the fallen arrow, then gave chase.

He continued running along a marked trail when a second mark appeared a few yards away. Again, Jordie followed, paused a couple of yards away, nocked his arrow on his bow, followed the target, and aimed.

Arrowsmith silently watched. He held his breath, remained still, and whispered to himself, "C'mon, son, breathe, aim, and shoot."

Jordie focused, released, and hit the bull's eye. His arrow lodged in the center of the mark before the target lost his footing and stumbled backward, cursing a string of French expletives.

Forgetting himself, Arrowsmith shouted for joy, leaped out of the bushes, and ran towards a startled Jordie. He picked him up, hoisted him onto his shoulders, and did a celebratory dance. Jordie was grinning from ear to ear because he had finally hit a moving object.

Meanwhile, the targets walked out of the thickets, both carrying wooden shields. One shield had an arrow lodged in its center.

"Well done, Jordan," Jean Luc said. "Your aim is much better."

"Good hit, monsieur; you even knocked me over," Pierre grumbled but winked at Jordie with a smile.

Then both men glared at Arrowsmith.

"Arrowsmith, you were supposed to stay hidden so Jordie can continue his training," Jean Luc said.

"Sorry, I got carried away. Tis not every day my... Jordie hits a moving target."

Jean Luc just shook his head in resignation. It was futile trying to run practice sessions with Jordie when Arrowsmith interrupted their training every time Jordie was successful at anything. But Jean Luc could not begrudge Arrowsmith his pride or his joy.

"When can I shoot arrows from a horse?" Jordie asked.

"When you can master riding a horse. Then we can combine both skills," Arrowsmith replied.

"I'm hungry. Can we get something to eat now?" Jordie asked.

"You are always hungry," Pierre chuckled as the group began walking towards the safe house.

"I think tis best we return before your Ma sends men to find you," Arrowsmith said as he lowered Jordie to the ground. They all knew Beth worried if Jordie was gone too long.

Jordie instinctively took Arrowsmith's hand as they walked, and Arrowsmith felt a tug on his heartstrings with the gesture. If only Jordie's mother trusted him as well, he would be the happiest man alive.

"Mama will not miss me today. She is going to be busy spending time with Carrington at the house," Jordie said.

"Who is Carrington?" Arrowsmith asked, not liking the rising tide of jealousy he felt.

"He helps Ma sometimes."

Arrowsmith glanced at Pierre, who just shrugged his shoulders. Then Arrowsmith looked at Jean Luc.

Jean Luc said, "He is Beth's solicitor."

"Jordie, why is Carrington coming to the house today?" Arrowsmith asked.

"Ma said something about selling things so we can move."

Arrowsmith's spine went rigid at that thought. Beth was moving, and she didn't tell him?

Sale Day

AT 1 PM, THE VULTURES arrived to pick at the remnants of Beth's life. Despite it being a discreet auction, all the gentry showed up in full force but not for support or a show of empathy. They came purely for sport, like sharks circling at the scent of blood. It was not enough they turned a blind eye to Beth's abuse for years; now they sought revenge against a dead man they all hated. Unfortunately, the one to suffer was Beth. She remained seated in the drawing room, sipping tea and not saying a word as people perused the items on sale.

"Well, my dear, I pity what has happened to you. All this could have been avoided if you had pursued a relationship with me instead of making a hasty union with James," Lord Lemington now hovered over her seat, smirking and stuffing his face with an apple tart.

Beth thought he had changed little since their fateful dance all those years ago. He was still full of self-importance, although now he was a little rounder around his middle and had a jaundiced pallor. He resembled a lemon tart. "Lemon tart full of farts" popped into her head for some unknown reason. Beth caught her chortles and swallowed them deep down into her throat.

"Had you not abandoned me at that dance, you might have escaped this public spectacle and ridicule," Lemington said.

"Moofy, I'm bored. 'Tis nothing here but garbage. Can we leave now?" Cora Lemington said, sidling up beside her husband.

"You call him Moofy?" Beth raised her eyebrow and snorted with an incredulous look.

Cora blushed when people turned to stare, then her face went purple.

Beth thought she resembled a pudding. How fitting, a lemon tart married to a purple pudding. Beth could not contain her mirth at her observation, and whether it was the nerves or the stress, she knew not, but she burst into a fit of giggles.

It outraged Cora that Beth was laughing at her. She unleashed her own set-down. "Yes, he's my Moofy, and you're just jealous because you're practically destitute—"

"Cora, do not get so worked up," Lemington warned his wife, trying to rein in her outburst. She was attracting attention. But Cora would not be waylaid.

"Everyone knows Davenport carried on with other women in this house, and you allowed it because you are a vile, unscrupulous woman!" Cora hissed.

"Cora, stop this at once," Lemington snapped.

"I will not!" Cora stomped her foot. "Look at her laughing at us when she is a harlot. Why, she most likely slept with several men at the scandalous house parties held here."

Beth froze and inhaled sharply at the accusation. In this spectator sport, she was an unwilling actor thrust center stage. If this was the past, Beth would let the slight go and crawl back into her corner like a frightened mouse. But she was different now, and this new version was not about to let sleeping dogs lie. She had spent seven years surrounded by vile creatures like the ones currently traipsing through the house, the same people who stood idly by while James and his cronies wreaked havoc. But not today. She was not putting up with it any longer.

Before Cora could speak another word, Beth stood and shouted, "Shut your mouth!"

Cora was stunned and closed her mouth.

But Beth was not finished. Oh no, far from it. After years of keeping quiet with her head down, turning the other cheek, she was done.

"You dare call me unscrupulous?" Beth hissed. "Why don't you tell Moofy over here how you've been carrying on with Lord Linley over there." Beth pointed her index finger at Lord Linley, who was examining a vase.

The crowd gasped, and Cora paled. Lord Linley almost dropped the vase.

"You lie!" Cora shrieked.

"Do I?" Beth smirked. "Then why does your son have the same birthmark that Lord Linley has on his buttocks?"

Cora gave herself away when she replied, "How do you know about Linley's birthmark?" She realized her mistake when she saw the scandalized expressions on the faces of many in the room.

Lemington dropped his half-eaten apple tart, yelled, "You son of a bitch!" and punched Lord Linley. A scuffle ensued with screeching women caught in the affray.

But Beth was nowhere near finished. She knew every dirty little secret the gentry hid behind closed doors.

She addressed the occupants of the room. "Do not act so smug, or I will start divulging all your misdeeds as well. Who should I start with next?" She took a turn about the room, tapping her index finger on her chin. "Let me see now..." She looked as if she was about to choose her next victim.

Some people were scurrying for the door. Guilty!

"You will stop these heinous accusations right now!" Lemington snarled and pushed her from behind.

Beth stumbled and righted herself, preventing her fall. She whipped around just in time to see Lemington coming at her again. This time his fist was clenched. Beth froze momentarily as she watched him approach her in a hostile manner. Then she remembered something Clarissa had taught her. Beth clenched one hand into a fist, then she pointed her index finger and middle finger at Lemington. He stepped closer with his arm raised, but before he could do any damage, Beth shot her fist forward as both fingers stabbed him in the eyes.

Lemington stepped back and shouted in pain, rubbing his eyes. Half-blinded, he tried to swipe her with his arm.

He did not get far.

One minute, Lemington was there; the next moment, Beth was pushed behind an impenetrable human shield called Ewan Arrowsmith. She saw Lemington lifted off his feet by the scruff of his collar and thrown against a side table. The table could not bear his weight, and it crashed beneath him.

"Never raise a hand to Miss Wakefield again, or I'll sever it from your body." Arrowsmith spoke in a quiet voice laced with steel.

Lemington paled and, to save face, said, "This is outrageous. Cora! Get over here now and help me; we are leaving."

"'Tis not true, Moofy..." Cora whined as she shuffled towards her husband and tried to help him stand.

"Be quiet and stop calling me that ridiculous name," Lemington hissed.

What followed was a mass exodus of all remaining potential buyers. Every one of them was terrified lest the unhinged Widow Davenport would air all their little secrets. None made eye contact with her as they scurried out of the house.

Arrowsmith faced Beth, concern in his eyes. "Are you all right, love?"

"Yes, thank you, Ewan, I am fine. But ah, what are you doing here?"

"You tell me, Beth." He clenched his jaw. "When were you going to tell me you were moving?"

She looked confused. "I am not moving, and it does not concern you."

Arrowsmith glared at her. "Everything about you and Jordie concerns me."

Carrington chose that moment to enter the room. "What on earth happened? Why is there a stampede of people leaving?"

"Sorry, Carrington, I could not stand them any longer," Beth replied.

"But you need them, Beth; who will buy these things now?"

Arrowsmith tensed, not liking the way Carrington called Beth by her given name. He wondered who Carrington was to Beth. He did not like that Carrington was also young and handsome. Not a hair out of place. Arrowsmith had the urge to ruffle his hair and drag him across the carpet, hoping to crease his pristine coat.

Arrowsmith placed an arm around Beth's waist and pulled her closer. Carrington did not miss the possessive gesture as the two men sized one another up, both scowling.

"I do not believe we have been introduced," Carrington said to Arrowsmith.

"I am Beth's man," Arrowsmith replied.

Beth was trapped between a stand-off, and fortunately, Jordie came running in before the two men grappled on the carpet.

"Mama, I hit a target with my bow and arrow!"

She moved out of Arrowsmith's arm and hugged Jordie. "Well done, Jordie. I am so proud of you."

"There are a lot of apple tarts in the kitchen; can I eat some?"

"Of course you can, just don't make a mess and keep out of Cook's way."

Jordie ran back out to the kitchen, licking his lips.

Carrington and Arrowsmith had not moved. Both men glowered at one another.

"Carrington, I thank you for all your help. If you do not mind, I would like a private word with Ewan."

He glared at Arrowsmith, and Arrowsmith smirked and gave him a miniature wave.

"All right. I will return to my office, but if you need me, Beth, just send a missive and I will be here."

"Thank you, I appreciate it, Carrington."

Carrington shot one last glare at Arrowsmith, grabbed his hat, and walked out the door.

Beth did not know what just happened, but it was high time she stopped Arrowsmith from making sweeping declarations about their relationship in public.

She turned to give him a piece of her mind and was dragged into the study instead, Arrowsmith's hand firmly clasping hers. Once inside, he shut and locked the door.

He growled, "Who is that man to you?"

"He is my solicitor."

"And?"

"And nothing, that is all."

"Why does he call you Beth?"

"I gave him leave to call me that."

"Not anymore."

"What do you mean?" She frowned.

"He is to call you Miss Wakefield and nothing else from now on, and I will be present should you need to speak to him again."

"That is preposterous!"

"He wants you, Beth."

"I beg your pardon?" She scoffed.

"Trust me, Beth, I am a man, and I can tell when a man wants a woman, and that man wants you."

"He is just my solicitor, Ewan; the only thing he wants is to keep me from becoming a pauper!"

"What do you mean?"

Beth sighed and decided it was time to tell him the truth.

"Davenport could not sire children. He agreed to marry me so he had an heir."

Arrowsmith moved in closer and said, "Go on."

"Jordie is his heir, but Davenport left him nothing but this debt-riddled estate."

Arrowsmith muttered, "Sounds like something that bastard would do."

"If I can sell off most of the things in this house, we may be able to pay off some of the debt so Jordie can keep his inheritance."

"Jordie will nae need it. He will inherit what I own," Arrowsmith replied.

"But he is Davenport's heir."

"He is my heir. He is my son."

"But if it comes out that we had him out of wedlock..."

"He is my son, Beth, and I will not have another man's name or estate attached to him."

"But think of the scandal, Ewan."

"Many are born on the wrong side of the blanket, Beth. All that matters is Jordie has something other than debt to worry about."

"But Jordie will lose Davenport's estate. I want him to have something to prove that we beat Davenport in the end."

"Beth, the best revenge is for Davenport's estate to go to the Crown so the world kens he died impoverished and with no heir."

Beth paused and knew Ewan was right. The fitting revenge was to let it all go. She stared at Ewan, seeing the merit of his reasoning, and she nodded in agreement.

They were silent for several moments.

"Now to our next issue. I want you to get rid of Carrington. You do not need him."

Beth sighed. "Ewan, will you stop with this obsession with Carrington? That man helped me when I had no one. He arranged for my escape, and he helps many women in similar circumstances. He deserves respect."

Arrowsmith grimaced at the reminder that he was not there for Beth when she needed him the most.

"Fine. I will be more polite in future. But Beth, that disgustingly handsome man will try to steal you away if you are not careful. But there's a problem with his plan."

Beth rolled her eyes, indulging his delusion. "And what is that, Ewan?"

"You are mine!" With those words, his lips came down on hers, and lord help her, Beth did not care one iota.

Beth was drowning in the sensation of being this close and secluded with Arrowsmith. Her spine started tingling, her breathing was shallow. Arrowsmith kept his pressure on her lips. Then his hands roamed her body.

It was strange that having Arrowsmith so close did not scare her at all. She was safe. And now other feelings invaded... a physical need so powerful she wanted to keep Arrowsmith close to her for all time.

Within seconds, Arrowsmith's deft hands were on her bare flesh. He had parted the top of her gown, exposing a breast. Her eyes glazed over as his hot mouth enclosed a nipple and he suckled her. Beth moaned in pleasure. It had been so long since she felt this.

She writhed under his ministrations. She felt her kirtle being lifted, then Ewan's palm was massaging her heat, adding pressure to her core. It was a relentless onslaught as he lay siege to her body.

Arrowsmith had lost all sense of propriety. Knowing that Carrington wanted his woman unleashed a possessiveness inside of him. He wanted to claim Beth and declare to the world she was his and only his. He knew he was going about it the wrong way, but he could not care less. He wanted inside her so badly, to fuse her body to his and bind her heart forever. By the moans and panting coming from Beth, he knew she was close to losing all control.

Arrowsmith was so close to taking her right there on the floor when he came to his senses. He did not want to make love to her on some worn carpet in Davenport's sullied home. No, he wanted her in their own home, with his ring on her finger so she could not leave him.

Arrowsmith pulled away, trying to calm his breathing. He was hard as stone, but he knew he could not debase her this way. Too much of

that had gone on in this house. She deserved only the best from now
on.

"I canna do this Beth, not like this. I am sorry, love."

Beth felt embarrassed and wanton. She thought Arrowsmith must
be disgusted with her. She thought about her scars. Maybe he saw them.
She bit her lip and nodded. How could she forget about her hideous
scars?

"I am sorry, Ewan. I do not know what came over me. If you will
excuse me, I must attend to something urgently."

Beth righted her clothing, opened the study door, and fled.

She heard Arrowsmith calling after her, but she would not look
back. She found Jordie and pulled him close to her; he was her shield.
She needed to keep a greater distance between her and Ewan from now
on.

Chapter 8 – Family Ties

Two weeks later, Arrowsmith felt like he was still pushing dung uphill and getting nowhere fast. Since that day in the study, he could not get a foot in with Beth. She remained closed off again. She kept the conversation to a bare minimum and only relating to the estate and Jordie. The one good thing was they at least agreed on letting Davenport's estate revert to the Crown. Arrowsmith saw to it immediately. He wanted Beth and Jordie free of any encumbrances or memories that reminded them of Davenport.

That afternoon, Beth and Arrowsmith agreed to tell Jordie the truth. Beth was going to bring Jordie to his residence in town, and he paced the hallway, nervous and waiting for them.

There was a knock at the door, and Arrowsmith ran to answer it immediately.

When he opened the door, Beth and Jordie stood on the threshold of his home, a home he hoped they would share once they moved out of Davenport's estate. But as with everything else, he had yet to broach that topic with Beth. One step at a time, he thought.

He ushered them inside. "Welcome to my home."

Beth was impressed with the size of the house. "Thank you." She blushed when Arrowsmith took their coats and hung them by the door. He moved them down the hallway.

"I have refreshments served."

He led them to a large room with opulent décor but that still looked quite masculine.

Jordie's face lit up when he saw a large array of food and pastries. "Look, Mama, have you ever seen so much food?"

Arrowsmith smiled. "I was not sure what you preferred, so I arranged for a bit of everything."

Within minutes, they were seated enjoying light refreshments.

"This is a lovely home, Ewan, and thank you for going to so much trouble with refreshments," Beth said.

"'Tis my pleasure, sweeting."

"Mr. Arrowsmith, can I come and visit you more often?" Jordie asked and bit into his second berry tart.

Arrowsmith chuckled. "Well, Jordie, that's what your ma and I need to discuss with you."

"Jordie, please pay attention; this is very important," Beth said.

"All right, what do you need to tell me?" Jordie swallowed the last bite of his pastry, wiped his mouth and hands on a napkin, and sat down between them.

"Many years ago, before you were born, Mr. Arrowsmith and I knew each other."

Jordie sat up straighter. "Did you? But how?"

"We ah... courted for a while," Arrowsmith replied.

"Before Mama met my Pa?" Jordie asked.

"Aye."

He frowned. "What happened?"

"We parted ways and never thought we would see each other again," Beth replied.

"But you are both here now. This is good."

"Why?" Beth asked.

"Do you still like my ma?" Jordie asked Arrowsmith.

"Aye, I do, verra much."

"Then why do you not marry her? She needs a good man, and I want brothers."

Arrowsmith almost choked on his drink. He coughed and spluttered.

"Jordie, 'tis not polite to say such things," Beth scolded him out of embarrassment.

Jordie was quiet for a moment, then he said to Arrowsmith, "My Pa, he was not a good man. He was mean to my mama. I did not like that about him."

"Aye, 'tis not right for a man to hurt a woman. When you become a man, you make sure you are nothing like him," Arrowsmith said.

"I am already a man, and I am going to be like you," Jordie replied.

Beth's eyes glistened with unshed tears whilst Arrowsmith choked down the lump in his throat.

"So, will you marry my mama so you can be my father?" Jordie asked, with hope in his eyes.

Beth inhaled a sharp breath then said, "Jordie, that is what we wanted to talk to you about. Mr. Arrowsmith is your real father."

"What?"

"Aye, son, I am your father." Arrowsmith held his breath, watching the different expressions play on Jordie's face. It went from a frown to confusion and then an enormous grin.

Jordie launched himself at Arrowsmith and hugged him tightly. Then he burst into tears.

"Och, son, dinnae cry, 'tis all right." Arrowsmith held him and tried to soothe him.

"I... I always wished... I was your real son. I used to pretend... that you were my father, and you loved me," Jordie sobbed.

Arrowsmith felt it pierce his soul, and he said with a scratchy voice, "I love you, Jordie, from the first moment I saw you, I loved you."

Beth was openly weeping now.

Arrowsmith reached out and pulled her into his side. She also wrapped her arms around Jordie. The three of them huddled together, filled with emotion.

The next few days went without a hitch as the three of them worked on their relationship. Beth remained stand-offish, but that made Arrowsmith more determined.

And then disaster hit by way of a storm and misunderstanding. The carnage it left in its wake left both parties feeling raw and broken.

The Storm

BETH FOUND IT INCREASINGLY difficult to keep her distance from Ewan. He was everywhere with Jordie, at the Cove, the safe house, visiting Clarissa and Dalziel Robertson, talking to her good friends Jean-Luc and Pierre, even down the main street. Her resolve was slowly eroding, and she had no protection against Ewan Arrowsmith's determination. When the man decided on a course, he stuck to it, and right now, his mission was to break down her walls.

The final straw came when Beth discovered he had arranged for her and Jordie to move into his house. Beth was fuming when Jordie came home excited because Arrowsmith had already shown him his room.

A storm was brewing, but Beth was so angry she traipsed through town in the pouring rain to Arrowsmith's house. She was so furious she failed to stop and think about what she was doing. She barged her way into Arrowsmith's home, sopping wet.

It never occurred to her he was not alone until she heard raised voices in the sitting room. It also never occurred to her that his visitor was a scantily clad woman sitting on his lap while he was bare-chested.

Arrowsmith looked shocked. He stood immediately and pushed the woman away. "Beth!"

"Too late," she rasped. Beth felt it then, that deep rumbling thunder within. She was back in Davenport's salacious world again. All her insecurities flooded back. Arrowsmith... seven years he had women, he probably still had women, mistresses, courtesans. He was never really hers at all. Everything was an act. Just like her late husband. They were all the same.

She paled, turned on her heel, and ran.

"Beth! Wait, 'tis not what it looks like, love, please, wait!"

"No, I should not have come," she yelled over her shoulder.

She opened the door and ran out into the storm. Only she did not go home. She headed for Clarissa's beachside cottage where Martin and Ruth lived. She needed their wise counsel, and she needed a place where Arrowsmith could not find her. Then she was going to make a bloody plan for her and Jordie that did not include him. She was done, so incredibly done with men and their lies.

She heard Ewan cursing in the distance, trying to get his shoes on until she heard angry voices as he argued with someone. She blocked it all out and disappeared into the night.

Her tears fell freely now, mingled with the rain to purge the darkness and purify her soul.

Macbeth's Castle, Dunsinane, Scotland – *One month later*

ARROWSMITH WAS DEPRESSED. No matter how hard he tried, he could not get Beth to speak to him. She never prevented him from seeing his son, but she made sure Martin accompanied Jordie in her place. He had not seen her at all; instead, she sent messages through other people. He was fast losing his patience with her.

That woman she saw was an old flame who arrived unannounced and tried to seduce him. If Beth had not run off, she would have noticed Arrowsmith was trying to push her away. *They had been arguing, for crying out loud.* The fact Beth had such little trust in him spoke volumes of what she suffered under Davenport.

But Arrowsmith was not sure how long he could be held at bay. It was hurting his pride that he had to keep chasing her down. Feeling despondent, he answered a call from King Macbeth to see to some business. And so Arrowsmith was currently sitting in Macbeth's private chamber in Scotland and thinking about Beth... again.

Macbeth raised an eyebrow and said, "Arrowsmith, I have kenned you for many years, and I sense all is not well with you?"

Arrowsmith remained silent.

"'Tis a woman, no doubt... they can be fickle creatures. But if she's a good one, loyal and strong of character, dinnae let her slip through your fingers." Macbeth picked at some grapes on his platter.

"With respect, Your Majesty, all is well with me," Arrowsmith replied curtly.

"And yet it is not."

Arrowsmith gritted his teeth. "Are you questioning my ability to do my duty, Your Majesty?"

"No, I am questioning your ability to see what is directly in front of your face."

Arrowsmith tensed, having no intention to discuss his personal life. But Macbeth persisted.

Macbeth changed tack. "Take Queen Gruoch and me if you will. When we married, it was by necessity. She was a mere political pawn. A victim of her late husband's over-ambition."

This piqued Arrowsmith's interest. It was rare for Macbeth to discuss his wife, whom he adored.

Arrowsmith asked, "How so?"

Macbeth leaned forward and said, "Her husband Gillecomgain killed my Da, Findlaech MacRuaridh. He plotted for years to ensure he had a straight line to the throne."

"Then how did you two end up married?"

"My Grand Da, King Malcolm the second, did nae like what Gillecomgain did and ordered him killed. He died by my hand. I wed his widow to retain my title."

Arrowsmith said, "I canna imagine the queen was pleased about it. No offense."

"Aye, it was not a good bargain for her. Gruoch had just survived a terrible marriage to a volatile man, then got lumped with me. She was verra hostile towards me until..."

"Until what, Your Majesty?"

"Till I realized I represented what she feared the most."

"What was that?"

Macbeth replied, "An ambitious, unfaithful man who cared nothing of a woman's heart."

They were silent for a moment as Macbeth stared out the window as if in deep thought. Macbeth took a deep breath then said, "So, I became the opposite of what she feared, and what I discovered was the greatest treasure. Do you ken what that is?"

Arrowsmith shook his head.

"I discovered my equal. My soul mate, the one woman I trust above all else and love above all else. I would die to protect her in a heartbeat. Even give up all of this to keep her with me."

"'Tis a special relationship you have, Your Majesty. I canna fault it."

"I suspect somewhere in your strategizing, Arrowsmith, you have missed the most important point of all."

"What is that?" Arrowsmith asked.

"You've found your great treasure, but you lack the courage to fight for it."

Arrowsmith stiffened at the insult. He was not a coward.

Macbeth continued, "James Davenport was a donkey's ass. He left a trail of destruction in his wake."

Arrowsmith spun around, surprised the king knew his predicament was about Beth.

Macbeth said, "But the one thing Davenport could not break was Elspeth. You ken why?"

Arrowsmith shook his head.

"Because Elspeth is a survivor. She has learned to bend, so she does nae break. If something threatens her, she passively resists it."

Arrowsmith nodded. Macbeth was right; that is exactly what Beth did. He sighed then admitted, "She will nae have me. I have tried. I dinnae think she places any significance in what I say anymore, let alone what any man says."

"Perhaps 'tis time you stopped speaking of your merits but showed her instead. It is not the words of a man that deem him trustworthy, Arrowsmith, it's his actions."

"Aye," Arrowsmith agreed.

Then Macbeth said, "Sometimes the greatest prize is the hardest to win, but win it you must, for there is no consolation for the one who stumbles at the first hurdle."

Arrowsmith paused and contemplated the wisest words he had heard in a long time. And right there, sitting on a heraldic seat at the table of the Red King, his path became clear, the clearest it had been in years. He was stumbling at the first hurdle.

He stood abruptly. "If you will excuse me, Your Majesty, I have a prize to win."

Macbeth just chuckled and said, "Aye, God speed, Arrowsmith."

Chapter 9 – The MacGregors

Beth the Fighter

The moment Arrowsmith left for Dunsinane, Beth and Jordie headed to Glenorchy, Scotland, for a brief reprieve. With Davenport's estate reverting to the Crown, Clarissa Robertson invited Beth and Jordie to stay with her family in Scotland for a few weeks. However, once they arrived, Amelia MacGregor insisted they stay at MacGregor Keep so Jordie could be around children his age.

During the two-week-long stay, Beth joined the clanswomen in their daily defence training sessions.

It was a crisp morning, and the MacGregor women and children were gathered by the loch.

Zala Fletcher did a roundhouse kick aimed directly at Beth. Beth ducked in time, grabbed Zala's ankle, and pushed back, causing Zala to lose her balance and land on her backside. Zala grumbled, then picked herself up, dusting off her trews.

"Yay!" the MacGregor children jumped up and down, clapping in celebration. They were a lively and boisterous group of spectators.

"Well done, Beth," Sorcha MacGregor yelled from the sidelines.

Beth beamed with pride, turned to her audience to curtsy when Zala kicked her backside. Beth lost balance and fell face-first into the water.

"No fair, Aunt Zala, she wasna looking," the children shouted in protest.

Amelia and Clarissa both burst out laughing as Beth rose from the water, her hair plastered across her face, spitting water out of her mouth. She smacked the surface in frustration as they fished her out.

Zala chuckled and said, "Never turn your back on the enemy, Beth." She turned to the children and said, "That goes for all of you as well. Dinnae celebrate too early."

"Blast! I was doing so well too," Beth grumbled.

"Aye, you knocked me off my feet; your skills are improving," Zala replied.

Someone handed Beth a drying cloth and blankets. Then it was Sorcha's turn to train at hand-to-hand combat with Zala, while Amelia and Clarissa practiced knife skills.

Watching the training sessions from the sidelines, Beth was in awe of the clanswomen. They trained as hard as the men. But she understood why. These were dangerous times in Scotland. Invaders came from everywhere, and women needed to learn to protect themselves and their children the same as their menfolk.

Jonet, the MacGregor chieftain's mother, told Beth stories of the old days when the women folk fought alongside their men to protect home and hearth. Jonet was proud that this new generation of women saw the benefit of learning combat skills. She was prouder still that she raised a son who encouraged it.

Beth wished she had these lessons early in life. If she had her time again, Davenport would have thought twice before laying a hand on her. She blessed the day she met Clarissa Robertson and the MacGregors.

Robertson House, Glenorchy, Scotland

DALZIEL ROBERTSON SAT at his desk in his study. His three-month-old baby son Cedric lay asleep in the crook of his arm.

His firstborn Jacob snoozed on the settee opposite Dalziel's desk, and sitting beside Jacob was Dalziel's wife, Clarissa.

He had moved his family to his Scottish home for a few weeks in lead-up to Christmas, leaving his English estate and the safe house in the hands of trusted associates.

It was late afternoon, Dalziel's favorite time of the day when Clarissa and his boys invaded his study so she could go over family matters with him.

Dalziel glanced at his wife, and his breath caught in his chest every time. She was the most beautiful, kindest woman he had ever known, and motherhood only deepened his love for her. Out in the world, he dealt with treachery and bloodshed, but all he needed was to come home to his family and he felt clean and whole again.

They were conversing in hushed whispers so as not to wake the children.

"Dalziel, we have to do something. I am worried about Beth and Arrowsmith," Clarissa said as she ran her fingers through Jacob's curly blonde hair.

"We will not do anything, Wife. Dinnae interfere. Beth will ken what to do in good time."

Clarissa rolled her eyes. "But I want her to be happy, and if there's a way I can bring that about—"

Dalziel gave her a warning look. "Ris, dinnae interfere and dinnae get Amelia or Zala to either. Things often go awry when you three stick your noses in other people's matters."

Clarissa gasped in outrage. "Since when? Our meddling has only ever produced favorable results."

"That's because Beiste, Brodie, and I smooth things over with the parties you meddle with."

Clarissa was indignant. "Name one time our interference has gone awry."

"How about when the three of you tried to match Kieran with the Murray widow? You almost got him killed."

"How were we supposed to know her husband wasn't dead and took offense to Kieran wooing his wife?"

"Or the time you convinced Lachlan to drink that love potion. Now the woman he fancies willna have anything to do with him."

"It wasn't my fault it upset his stomach, and he vomited on her."

"Ris! It *was* your fault. I will say it again, sweeting, please do not trifle with Beth or Arrowsmith."

Clarissa huffed. "Very well then, we won't. However, Beth wants to know if Arrowsmith is coming for Christmas at the MacGregors."

"Why? Is she still avoiding him?" Dalziel raised his eyebrow.

"Yes, she thinks it best they focus on Jordie and not bring up the past. She is talking of traveling to France for a few weeks."

Dalziel thought on that a while then replied, "Arrowsmith has work to do for Macbeth in the South. There is no chance he would make it to Glenorchy in time for Christmas."

"Then that will be a great relief for Beth. I will tell her 'tis safe to remain as Arrowsmith cannot make it."

"Aye, 'tis a good idea." Dalziel walked over and stood beside the settee. "Now let's get these bairns to bed because I need to play with my wife." He gazed at her with intensity.

Clarissa took a sharp intake of breath and returned a sultry smile.

The following morning, Dalziel penned a missive to Ewan Arrowsmith, his trusted friend in Northumbria. The message was brief: "Come for Christmas. Beth and Jordie are here."

He penned a second missive, this time to the king of Scotland. He requested a special marriage license.

When both missives were sent, Dalziel chuckled to himself. Clarissa was an amateur. Dalziel was a master when it came to meddling in other people's lives.

1046 - Christmas Day, MacGregor Keep

ARROWSMITH STEPPED into the warmth of the Great Hall at MacGregor Keep, and he was livid. He had ridden hard to arrive that night—through bloody snow and sleet—to be here in case his vixen tried to escape him again. Beth had given him the runaround for the last time. If it were not for Dalziel's missive, Arrowsmith would still be in Northumbria wondering where Jordie and his stubborn mother had hied off to. This time he was staying put with the MacGregor clan, which he now considered part of his own family, and he was going to wear her down until she could not escape.

He was growling and striding towards Beth, who was surprised to see him. He stalked closer when three women blocked his way. He gritted his teeth; it was Clarissa Robertson, Amelia MacGregor, and Zala Fletcher. The three most interfering women he had ever had the misfortune to encounter. It was their fault Beth could avoid him so well.

Amelia stood with her hands on her hips, about to warn him off, when Beiste appeared at her side and hauled her over his shoulder. He greeted Ewan with a handshake and said, "Do what you came to do."

"Beiste! I was talking," Amelia scolded.

"Hush, love, 'tis not your concern." They could be heard bickering down the hall.

Clarissa was the next line of defence and about to say something when she shrieked in surprise as Dalziel picked her up and carried her off as well.

"Dalziel Robertson, you lied to me," she hissed.

Dalziel chuckled and replied, "You have much to learn, wife."

That left only one more gatekeeper, and she was formidable. Zala terrified Arrowsmith because the blasted woman could grapple, and if he lowered his guard, he could lose his ability to sire more children.

Arrowsmith said, "Please move, I need to see to my woman."

"Oh no, you will not get past me, Rowie." Zala stood with her arms folded, daring him to make a move. "And dinnae think Brodie will help you. Brodie is in full agreement—" Zala yelped as she also disappeared out of view, now dangling over Brodie's shoulder.

"Brodie Fletcher! You put me down right now."

He spanked her bottom and said, "I'll do no such thing, wench, and since when have I ever agreed with you?" Brodie chortled and winked at Arrowsmith as he passed by.

Jordie appeared and threw himself at Arrowsmith. His face split into a wide grin.

Arrowsmith crouched down and hugged his son. They spoke quiet words before Jordie nodded, then returned to play with the other children.

Arrowsmith stood and now stared directly at his wife. Because that is what she was, his wife. She just did not know it yet.

"Beth, 'tis time you ceased hiding from me. I need you to listen to what I have to say."

Silence descended over the hall as people observed with avid fascination the drama unfolding. They continued to eat, never taking their eyes off the couple at the front table.

At one point, a man called for a cup of mead, and several people shushed him, straining their ears to better hear the conversation.

Beth blushed with embarrassment at all the attention now on her. "You have nothing to say that I want to hear, Ewan."

"What you saw that night was not what you think."

"It does not matter. You have every right to take whatever lover you please."

The sound of people murmuring amongst themselves and repeating Beth's words down the line to others annoyed him.

Arrowsmith turned around and glared at everyone. They quickly got back to minding their own business, acting as if they were not listening in. Arrowsmith then whipped his head back to Beth. "Can we please go talk somewhere private?"

Beth shook her head as she stood abruptly and ran towards the stairwell.

"Dammit, Beth!" Arrowsmith took off after her.

She made it to the landing of the guest wing and sprinted for her chamber.

Arrowsmith was not far behind. He yelled, "Beth, stop running from me."

She made it inside the room and tried to close the door, but he put his foot in front of it to stop her from closing it. He stood across the threshold and refused to budge.

"Go away! Why are you even here? Leave me be," she shouted and tried to push him away.

He stood firm. "I'm not leaving you, Beth. No matter how many times you push me away, I'll keep coming back."

"Why are you doing this, Ewan?" she said in frustration.

"Because I love you, Beth. I never stopped loving you, and I want a future with you."

She paused and looked directly at him, trying to find out the truth of his words.

"You love me?"

"Aye, always, and I want a life with you and Jordie more than you can ever imagine."

Beth gave up trying to move the mountain standing in her doorway. She stepped away and sat on the bed, exhausted.

Arrowsmith remained standing on the threshold. "May I please come in, Beth? I want to talk to you inside, but if you prefer, I can do it from here."

Beth sighed and said, "'Tis not like I can move your enormous boulder of a backside."

Arrowsmith sighed, crossed the threshold, and closed the door.

Lost

ARROWSMITH MOVED ABOUT the chamber, started the fire to warm the room, and removed his sodden cloak, hanging it by the mantlepiece.

Beth retrieved a blanket and handed it to him with a cloth to dry his hair. The gesture touched Arrowsmith, and he thanked her. She watched him and remembered a time years ago when he had done the same thing, in a small bothy in the woods the night Jordie was conceived.

When Arrowsmith turned to face her, he had the blanket wrapped around him and a feral glint in his eye. "'Tis time we talked about that woman you saw in my house."

"I do not want to talk about her." Beth stood and started pacing.

"Beth, I need to explain. Aye, she was a past lover, but I ended it long ago because she wanted more than I could give. I did not invite her. She barged into my home not long before you did, trying to rekindle a flame long gone."

"I do not want to know, Ewan." Beth covered her ears.

Arrowsmith stood before her and removed her hands from her ears. His eyes softened, and he said, "Beth, please believe me. I was sitting by the fire; next thing I ken she had snuck in. If you looked closely, you would have seen I was trying to push her away."

Beth remained tense, her head down, listening and taking it all in. Then she asked, "Have you been with other women since you saw me again at the safe house?"

"None, I swear it."

"What about in the time we were apart?" Her voice wavered.

Arrowsmith whispered, "Dinnae ask me questions you ken you will not like the answer to."

Beth pulled herself out of his arms. "I think you better leave."

Arrowsmith's voice was gentle when he said, "Dinnae judge me for a time I thought you left me. I mourned you, Beth, but I should never have believed Robert. I regret that more than anything."

Beth could not help the jealousy that crept in. He sought intimacy with others; they were most likely beautiful. While she lived a nightmare.

"I have not lived like a monk, Beth, and I'm sorry for it. But please understand, I thought you were married, that you had chosen someone else over me, that you loved another man. I regret that I did not trust in us more than I trusted Robert."

"These women, did you love them, Ewan? Were they... pretty?" Beth asked.

Arrowsmith saw the vulnerability in her eyes, and he gritted his teeth because he knew the only thing he could offer her was the truth.

He took a deep breath and said, "I've had exactly three lovers in the past seven years. The first reminded me of you. She wanted marriage and bairns, but I did not love her. I tried, but she was not my dream. In the end, I could offer her nothing, and she moved on to another."

Beth felt heartsick to hear that he had tried to love another. But she simply nodded.

Arrowsmith continued, "The second was a highborn lady of the royal court. She helped fill a void of loneliness for a time. When the king elevated my position, she pushed for marriage. Only then did she see me as worthy of her attention. But I refused because, in the end, she was not my dream."

This time Beth just bit her lip and nodded again.

Arrowsmith pushed on. "The third turned out to be a spy, and she was the one who almost got you and Clarissa killed at the safe house. Again, my biggest regret. So, there you have it. That's the lascivious history of Ewan Arrowsmith. Contrary to what you may think, I didnae have a harem of women, and more often than not I was alone, but still, I canna change the past."

Beth took a sharp intake of breath, then remained silent and contemplative. She had asked, and he had given her the truth. Beth decided the kindest thing she could do was leave the past behind and Arrowsmith with it.

Arrowsmith began to worry when Beth did not say a word or even react. Panic set in, and he decided to plead his case again. "Beth, please understand. I believed you were lost to me."

Beth replied in a whisper, "I am still lost, Ewan. And I don't think I'll ever be found."

She stood and ran for the door, but he caught her and gently held her.

"Let me go!" she shouted. She fought him like a wildcat, and Ewan dodged her hits and scratches and tried to calm her.

"Don't you see, Ewan? We cannot have what we lost! I am not the same." With those words, Beth crumpled in his arms and wept.

Arrowsmith pulled her close. "Neither am I, sweeting. We cannae change the past, but we've been given a second chance. We have the power to do things differently right now. We still have a future, Beth!"

Arrowsmith picked her up. He sat on the bed and placed her on his lap.

Beth sobbed in his arms and said, "Seven years, Ewan. I've missed you for seven years."

"You're breaking my heart, mo leannan."

Beth allowed the tears to flow as she let out heart-wrenching sobs. She clung to him like he was a lifeline amid a stormy sea.

Arrowsmith whispered over and over, "I will never leave you, Beth. I love you. I have always loved you, and I will move heaven and earth to keep you." He cupped her face in his palms so he could look at her directly. "Our lives begin today. All we have is this moment. One day at a time, Beth. Can you give me that?"

Beth nodded. Her eyes were awash with tears when she pleaded with him, "Do not let me go, Ewan, never let me go."

"Never. You are mine, and I hold on to what is mine."

For the first time in years, Beth allowed herself to fall, trusting that Ewan would catch her.

Arrowsmith felt the shift and the realization that he finally had Beth back. It humbled him. They clung to each other for comfort and solace in the knowledge they would never be apart again.

After a short time had elapsed in silence, Arrowsmith said, "I want you as my wife, Beth. I want you in my bed every night. I want to see you round with more of our bairns in your belly. I want you and Jordie under my roof in my home here in Scotland where I can love and protect you both."

Beth's eyes shone with hope, and she nodded.

"Beth, you have always been my dream." His last words were a plea as his lips descended on hers.

Beth melted. Tears were streaming down her face at the promise that she could share his dream too. One day at a time. All resistance faded as she lost herself in the kiss.

Arrowsmith was in heaven. Finally, he had Beth in his arms again, and all was right with the world. If only the annoying shuffling sound from the hallway would stop, he thought.

Eavesdroppers

"I CANNA HEAR ANYTHING," Amelia whispered whilst her ear was up against the door of Beth's bedchamber.

"Move, let me see." Zala scuttled around her, crouched down, and tried to look through the keyhole. "There's something in the way. I canna see inside."

"Do you think he is kissing her?" Clarissa asked. "I can hear a moaning sound."

"That better be all he is doing. I still need to check his man parts," Amelia replied with a scowl.

"You and your man parts. As if Beiste will let you near his cock." Zala snorted.

"Can you see anything yet?" Clarissa asked Zala. She was impatient and concerned for Beth.

"Wait... yes, I can see movement." Zala moved her eye closer to the keyhole.

The other two women held their breath and placed their ears against the door... when it opened, and they all tumbled inside the room.

"What the bloody hell are you doing? Can't a man kiss his woman without you three hovering about?" Arrowsmith growled.

Beth was still dazed, touching her lips, feeling them still tingling from Arrowsmith's attentions. She blushed when she saw the three women sprawled on the floor, then started giggling. She walked across and helped Arrowsmith pull them up.

When they were righted, Amelia glared at Arrowsmith and demanded he show her his man parts before he took any more sexual liberties with Beth.

Arrowsmith glowered at her.

Beth tried to stifle a laugh.

Zala rolled her eyes, and Clarissa said, "Oh, for crying out loud, Amie, that is not the point right now!"

"Then what exactly is the point? Why are you all here?" Arrowsmith glowered at the three of them.

"We want to make sure Beth is all right and you are not ravishing her," Amelia replied.

"As you can see, she is fine. As for ravishment, that is none of your concern." Arrowsmith shuffled the three of them out the door.

Amelia shouted, "Beth, if you want him gone, I will tell Beiste to do it. You ken I am the real authority around here."

Zala rolled her eyes, and Clarissa stifled a snort then cleared her throat.

"What? I am!" Amelia shouted with indignation at the two women beside her.

"Beth, do you want me gone?" Arrowsmith asked Beth while glaring at Amelia.

"No, 'tis all right, you can stay," Beth replied.

"See, she is fine. Now goodbye." Arrowsmith shut the door in their faces and locked it.

Chapter 10 – Mysterious

Beth and Arrowsmith emerged from the room and joined everyone in the hall for the rest of the Christmas meal. Jordie sat nearby, beaming with happiness.

Dalziel handed Arrowsmith two documents.

"These are the parchments?" Arrowsmith asked.

"Aye, 'tis your marriage license already signed by Macbeth. 'Twas officiated by proxy, and the other parchment you requested. This is a favor the king has never done for anyone else."

"Thank you, Dalziel. I owe you much," Arrowsmith said.

"You once saved my wife when I could not be there for her. 'Tis the least I can do for you," Dalziel replied, then walked away.

Beth asked, "What was all that about?"

Arrowsmith took a deep breath and replied, "I ken this may be too soon, but Dalziel arranged a marriage by proxy for us, signed by the king. These are our marriage papers."

"You mean we are already married, and you did not even ask me?"

"Aye, love. I wanted to prove that I never want to be without you. I want our family to be united."

"But what if I do not want to be married now? You have taken away my right to choose my own future. What happened to taking one day at a time?"

Arrowsmith sighed. "You do have the right to choose, Beth. Take this." He handed her the other parchment.

"What is this?"

"Annulment papers. It only needs your signature, and the marriage is annulled immediately."

Beth gasped in shock. "But how?"

"The king has never offered this to anyone else. Dalziel negotiated it on my behalf. It's to ensure that if you really dinnae want to be married to me, then you sign that parchment and take this marriage paper and rip it up. You have the power to end it at any time, and I will have no say. These are yours to hold for as long as you need." Arrowsmith handed her the marriage parchment as well.

"You had the king do this for me?" Beth asked in awe.

"Aye. I ken you have not had any control over your life, and my overbearing ways probably dinnae help. But I want you to ken that the power is always yours. Whether you choose to remain married to me or not, 'tis your decision to make, and I'll not interfere."

Beth held the parchments in her trembling hand and became overwhelmed with gratitude that Arrowsmith understood her reluctance. She wanted to be married to him above anything else, but she struggled with the feeling of being powerless for so long. This way he had given her exactly what she needed: the power to decide in her own time.

Arrowsmith began to feel increasingly uneasy given Beth's complete silence. "Love, I can see I have hurt you unintentionally. I am so sorry. Forget it. You're right. I am a brute and a lout, and I should not have done this. Dinnae worry, I will rip up the marriage papers; 'tis too much too soon." He reached for the parchments, but Beth clutched them to her chest.

"Ewan Arrowsmith, don't you dare take something this precious away from me!" she growled.

"Beth? But I dinnae ken—"

"You promised me you would never let me go. Is that still true?"

Arrowsmith gazed at Beth and whispered, "Aye. I promise."

"Good. Then I shall hold onto this forever. And the moment you rile my temper or do something boorish, I'll reconsider my decision. But until then, you are stuck with me as your wife!" She then gifted him with a broad smile.

The air left Arrowsmith's lungs, and he felt pure elation. "You will have me then as your husband?"

"Aye, you're mine!" Beth replied.

Arrowsmith grabbed her and kissed her in front of everyone. Then he shouted at the top of his lungs, "Everybody, let me introduce you to my wife!"

The room roared with approval.

He picked Jordie up so he stood on the chair between them. Then he shouted, "And this is our son!"

Everyone in the hall grinned and cheered.

Soon they were surrounded by elated MacGregor men offering congratulations and angry MacGregor women.

"What is the meaning of this?" Amelia asked.

"Beth and I are married by proxy. Dalziel arranged it with Macbeth. We are husband and wife now," Arrowsmith replied with a grin as he clasped Beth and Jordie's hands.

All the women looked shocked and then outraged.

"You canna do that! What about the wedding and the church vows?" Amelia asked.

"And the dress," Sorcha added.

"And the flowers," Iona and Izara said in unison.

"Not to mention the wedding feast," Jonet added. "You canna just decide these things for a woman's big day." Jonet was outraged to think Beth would not have a proper ceremony.

Clarissa just glared at Dalziel. "How could you rob Beth of a proper wedding?"

Dalziel suddenly looked contrite.

"That's right, Dalziel, in all your scheming you did not think about that, did you?" Clarissa raised an eyebrow.

"So typical of a man to take the best things away from a woman," Zala grumbled.

"What are you talking about, wife? You had two weddings with two dresses and everything!" Brodie replied.

"You're really married to Mama?" Jordie asked with tears glistening in his eyes.

"Aye, son," Arrowsmith rasped, choked up with emotion.

Jordie beamed with happiness as he hugged his parents, then leapt off the chair to join his friends.

Beth and Arrowsmith just gazed at one another with pure love. Their tender moment was interrupted when Amelia pulled Beth out of Arrowsmith's arms and said, "Beth is still getting a church wedding, and you canna see the bride until then. No sharing a room until I have checked your man parts."

"Over my dead body," Beiste MacGregor growled.

Everyone just rolled their eyes. They were used to this ongoing argument between the chieftain and his wife.

Once the Christmas feast was over, the women ushered Beth to a separate bedchamber, and Jordie stayed with his father.

Beth laughed when Arrowsmith muttered, "Bloody interfering women!"

Winter Rose

OVER THE NEXT TWO DAYS, the Keep was a hive of activity as they prepared for a simple wedding in the chapel and a light repast in the hall. Jordie was so excited he wanted to contribute his share, and he knew how to do it. His mother loved flowers, and he knew where he could get some fresh ones for her wedding day. He had seen some growing by the rowan tree in the woods.

Even though the weather was deathly cold, he wanted his mother to have Helleborus winter roses. They were the few flowers resilient enough to grow in winter. He had trekked out that way before with the other children and guardsmen, and as the weather was clear, he did not think it would take him long to gather some while everyone else was busy.

Jordie set out dressed warmly and ready to battle the cold. He had his sword and a pouch to gather the flowers. Halfway there, he had not expected the weather to change so rapidly.

The snow built up fast, and he was trying to maintain his bearings. It was a hard struggle, but he finally came upon the tree where they grew at the base. He picked several and carefully placed them in his pouch. Then he made his way back to the Keep. The only problem was when he turned around, everything looked exactly the same. He could not find his tracks or the direction in which he came.

He kept walking and saw nothing that looked familiar. Just white trees. Jordie felt colder as the snowstorm grew into a blizzard. He was lost. Jordie tried to find somewhere he could shelter until it passed. He was walking towards a fallen tree stump when the ground beneath him gave way, and he fell inside an old well. He shouted and landed awkwardly, twisting his ankle.

Jordie was in pain, and his leg throbbed. His teeth chattered with the icy winds. He was deathly cold and miserable. No one knew he was here. In his haste to surprise his parents, he had taken no precautions.

"Help!" he shouted. But no one could hear his tiny voice over mother nature's wintery roar.

Jordie huddled into a ball and shivered, but he held the winter rose carefully in his pouch.

"Help me please," he yelled. The blustering wind was his only response.

Worry

"AUNTY SORCHA, HAVE you seen Jordie? He went outside to get something, but he has nae come back," Colban MacGregor, Beiste's son, asked her. Thorfinn Fletcher stood beside him.

Sorcha was helping the women readying the chapel, but when she saw her nephews' worried faces, she stopped what she was doing.

"Have you asked the others?"

"Aye, but they all say he is probably around the Keep somewhere."

Sorcha put down the wreath she was making.

"All right, where did you last see him?"

Colban led Sorcha to the entranceway where he last saw Jordie. Sorcha did not like the look of the weather. She did a quick search of the surrounding area to no avail.

They came across Iona and Izara eating custard tarts. When Sorcha asked if they had seen Jordie, Iona replied, "Jordie wanted to pick flowers for his ma, but I told him it was too cold to go outside. He must be somewhere inside."

Sorcha tensed. The only place the flowers bloomed this time of year was near the rowan tree. She looked outside again and noticed a small pair of faded shoe prints heading out, but none coming back.

Sorcha grabbed her fur-lined cloak and warm plaid. Time was of the essence. If Jordie was still out there, he could freeze to death, and he did not know the way back.

"Colban, you listen to me well," Sorcha said.

Colban nodded his head in all seriousness.

"Go find your da and your uncles. Tell them Jordie is missing and to head for the rowan tree. Go!"

Colban took off to do her bidding.

"Thorfinn, go find your uncle, Kieran. Tell him to fetch Jordie's da from the armory and tell them to head to the rowan tree."

"Aye, Aunty," Thorfinn said and took off running.

"Izara, find your mathair, tell her to get Jordie's ma."

"Iona, tell your mathair to prepare. She will ken what I mean."

Both girls nodded, clasped each other's hands, and ran to find their mothers.

As soon as the children left, Sorcha rugged up, grabbed her bow and quiver, placed the hood over her head, and ran out into the winter blizzard. She prayed they found Jordie before he froze to death.

A Savior

JORDIE KNEW HE WAS going to die. He was so cold and exhausted. He could not feel his legs; they were so numb. He curled himself into a ball, but the icy cold moisture was seeping into his bones.

He called one more time. "Help," he said in a hoarse voice. His strength was waning. Then he heard a noise, a shuffling sound. Jordie looked up and saw a dark-haired man wearing a woollen plaid. He stood above the opening, but he did not look familiar.

"Dinnae move! I'm coming down to get you," the man shouted.

He was not alone because Jordie could hear him arguing with someone else.

"This is not part of the plan. What the bloody hell do you think you're doing?"

"We canna leave him here; he will die."

"What do we care about a MacGregor? Let the runt die."

"He's just a bairn. Lower the rope; I am going down to get him."

"Dinnae be a fool, leave him or you will get us all killed before we've even begun."

"Shut your mouth and hold the damned rope!"

It terrified Jordie they were going to leave him. He pleaded, "Please, mister, dinnae leave me here."

"I willna leave you, lad. I'm coming down."

Like a savior, the large man lowered himself down the hole via a rope. When he reached Jordie, he wrapped him in a warm blanket, then picked him up and tugged on the rope. Jordie felt himself ascending, but his eyes were already drooping.

The man nudged him awake and said, "Dinnae sleep, lad. Stay alert."

When they reached the top, Jordie saw another man with a hooded cloak. He scowled at Jordie.

"We need to get him to a healer; he's burning up with fever," his rescuer said.

"And how do you suggest we do that? Just walk right into the Keep and ask for the chieftain's wife?"

"There is someone else, an old crone. She lives near here. We can take him there."

The other man shook his head and grumbled as he stormed off to retrieve their horses.

Jordie was lifted again as the man carried him. He wanted to sleep, but his rescuer growled at him several times to stay awake.

Mysterious Highlander

THE HIGHLANDER STOOD on the threshold of a small cottage, cradling the child in his arms. The door opened, and a woman with white eyes and grey hair appeared. He'd heard them call her 'Morag.'

"Och, so ye have finally revealed yourself, Highlander," she said.

It confused him because he had never met her before. "I dinnae have time, old woman. The bairn needs help; he is half frozen."

Morag glanced down and realized he was carrying a wrapped bundle. She saw it was Jordie and ushered them inside. The Highlander helped her get Jordie dry and lay him on a cot by the fireplace, rugged up in warm blankets.

He stood and turned to leave when Morag grabbed his arm.

"You made the right decision today, Highlander. Your good deed will come full circle."

He pulled his arm away. "I dinnae need your predictions, witch. I have wasted precious time already."

"Tsk, so impatient. Ye best prepare for what is coming. Here," she said, holding out something for him.

"What is this for?" He stared at the tiny package.

"'Tis the difference between life and death," Morag replied.

He clenched his jaw, took it, and placed it in his pocket. He nodded, then stepped out into the bitter cold. His companion was waiting by the trees with the horses.

The Highlander walked a few paces when he saw a woman running up the path towards him. She had followed their trail. He froze when her hood dropped, revealing her face and their eyes locked. He inhaled a sharp breath, and so did she. He was still reeling from the sight of her when she pulled up a bow and a nocked arrow that was aimed right at him.

"Who are you and where is Jordie?" she demanded.

"If you mean the bairn I found in the snow, he is inside the cottage, lass."

"Then what are you doing here?" she snapped at him.

"'Tis none of your concern," he replied.

She kept her arrow trained on him. In the distance, he saw more men approaching. His companion growled, "We have to go now!"

It startled Sorcha, not realizing there was a man by the trees. She pointed her arrow in his direction. That was all the time the

Highlander needed. Before Sorcha knew what was happening, he had disarmed her and now held her bow and arrow in his hands.

Sorcha could hear Beiste and Brodie calling her name in the distance.

The Highlander looked at a point past her shoulder. He gritted his teeth then said, "Sorry, beauty, but I dinnae have time today. We shall meet again and become better acquainted."

Quicker than lightning, he threw her weapons aside, then his hand shot out. He pulled her hood down over her head, twirled her around, and pushed her into the snow. Then he sprinted for his horse.

By the time Sorcha untangled herself from her cloak, he had vanished.

"Damn it!" she swore. Sorcha was so angry with herself for allowing a man to best her by weaponizing her own cloak. She picked up her bow, cursed several times, and sprinted for the cottage.

BY THE TIME JORDIE came to, he was back in the Keep in his warm bed as his parents hovered over him. He tried to sit up, frantic that he lost the white roses, but he saw them sitting beside the bed and relaxed.

Amelia, Arrowsmith, and Beth took turns bringing his fever down throughout the night. By the following morning, Jordie's fever broke, and Amelia declared he would be all right. Arrowsmith was beside himself with worry and watched Beth take it all in her stride. He asked, "How did you do this alone all those years caring for our son?"

Beth replied, "Love, Ewan. Love bears all things and conquers all things."

THE HIGHLANDER WHO rescued Jordie saved his life. And everyone knew it. It was still a mystery who he was. Sorcha thought of him many times since their meeting. She had never met someone like him before. His deep blue eyes were piercing, and energy and raw vitality emanated from his very being. She felt an instant connection to him, and it confused her.

Chapter 11 – Love & Marriage

At Last

A day later, Beth and Arrowsmith wed in the chapel, with much fanfare. Beth proudly held the small bunch of white roses as a bouquet while Jordie stood beside Arrowsmith as his best man. The clan gathered for the celebration feast afterward, and there was much joy and laughter.

That night, Arrowsmith held Beth's hand and led her to the special bedchamber Amelia had prepared for the newlyweds. He carried her over the threshold, then placed her on her feet beside the bed.

Arrowsmith had waited for this moment for a lifetime. For seven long years, he thought he had lost her, his dream, and yet here she was, his radiant wife. The most beautiful woman he had ever known, bar none.

Beth felt somewhat embarrassed and untried. The last time they made love, they were young and full of promise. This time it was different. They had matured with time and life experiences. Beth's body was different, and so was Arrowsmith's. He was all muscle and hard-defined contours with battle scars. She wore scars of her own.

Arrowsmith gently removed her shift and took his fill. He raked her body with his eyes.

Under his penetrating gaze, Beth felt desired, beautiful, and wanton.

Arrowsmith noticed her breasts were still a handful; she was all curves with an hourglass figure. She was and always had been the most attractive woman, bar none. Then he saw the markings across her stomach. Blemished skin caused by callous hands. He wanted to kill Davenport. His body tensed. He clenched his fists and squeezed his eyes shut.

Beth took a step back, ashamed of her body. She bowed her head in embarrassment, biting her lip.

"Sweeting, look at me," Arrowsmith said. He placed his finger under her chin, tipped her head to meet his eyes. She tried to cover her scars with her hands, but Arrowsmith pushed them away and gently traced the scarred line with his fingers. "Dinnae hide from me. I love every inch of you; please dinnae cry."

"I know the scars are ugly."

Arrowsmith framed her face with his hands and gazed into her eyes. "Nothing about you is ugly, my love, nothing at all. I see only beauty and strength. I am angry that someone would dare harm you. I am ashamed because I was not there for you, love." He kissed her lips and savored the sweetness, then Arrowsmith knelt on the floor in front of her. He placed light kisses on her scars and scattered more along the length of the jagged skin across her belly.

She blushed and tried to step away, but Arrowsmith held her firmly in place.

"I have marks from when I was carrying Jordie," Beth murmured.

"Aye, and I love them all because they remind me you cradled my bairn inside you, kept him safe when I could not. And you will carry more of our bairns here, Beth, and that is a precious gift indeed."

As her tears flowed with the intimacy of this moment, Beth felt vulnerable and yet completely safe. Under his penetrating gaze, she felt desired and cherished. Wherever his eyes roamed, his hands, lips, and tongue followed. Beth gently ran her fingers through Arrowsmith's hair until the feeling of intimacy soon turned to something more. A passionate heat traveled throughout the length of her body with each caress.

Arrowsmith also felt the shift. From a gentle wildfire to a scorching inferno. He was rock hard. He kissed his way up the length of his wife's body, then stood in front of her as their breathing became ragged. He caressed her breasts with his calloused hands. His thumbs rubbing against her nipples, before he bent low and suckled her perfect peaks. This version of Beth was more refined, but he still knew his way around her body. Like a familiar second skin. Arrowsmith felt as if his heart would burst with overwhelming love.

He lifted her into his arms, and he walked them to the bed. Then he lay her down and went about reclaiming what was his, one kiss at a time.

Beth lost herself in a haze of euphoric pleasure as Arrowsmith lay naked above her, laving her breasts with his tongue. He spread her legs apart, his hand massaged her intimately as he continued to lavish attention on her nipples. His breathing became ragged as his passion increased. Beth gently caressed his skin, then reached down and gripped his hardened length. Arrowsmith groaned with pleasure as she caressed him with her hand. Their eyes met, their lips touched, and Beth knew she would love no other man for as long as she lived. He was finally hers, and she was his.

Arrowsmith pulled away and spread her legs wider so she could cradle his hips between her thighs. Beth felt his hardened length nudge against her center, and she was ready to be his again. No fear, no past tainting her memories. Just her first love consuming her and banishing the bitter memories of her past. She felt him push forward and enter her body one inch at a time. She gripped his hips with her hands, urging him to take her. Arrowsmith complied and thrust inside her to the hilt. Then began the slow dance of love as he filled her again and again, and she opened her body and her heart to him.

Arrowsmith was deep inside the woman he loved, and he felt complete for the first time in a long time. Beth's heated core enveloped him like a glove, and he was undone. He moved within her tight sheath, taking his pleasure as he gave her all of himself. He held nothing back. For the first time in years, Arrowsmith made love to the only woman he had ever loved, would ever love. He poured his heart and soul into Beth. When Beth climaxed, it stole the very breath from his lungs as he came deep inside her with a roar.

Pillow Talk

LATER THAT NIGHT AFTER Arrowsmith had pleasured his wife five more times, and she had drained him of not only his seed but also his energy, he grinned at the wanton minx lying in his arms with her head resting against his chest. They were speaking in hushed tones. Beth was gently drawing circles on his chest with her hand as Arrowsmith ran his fingers through her hair as they talked.

"When you left, I felt empty, bereft inside for the longest time. Nothing could fill the void; it hurt to even breathe most days," Arrowsmith said. "I held on to your sketches and paintings."

"You did not," she replied in disbelief.

"Aye, I did. Look in my boist."

She reached across him and pulled the pouch onto the bed. Inside was the painting of a couple embracing. It had faded a little, but the colors were still vivid.

She caressed it with her fingers. "I have not painted or sketched in years."

"Why not, sweeting? You have an exceptional talent."

Beth raised her head and kissed her husband on the lips, then she settled back against his chest and said, "From the day I was born, all I saw was vibrant color, everywhere. Then when I thought you were dead, the color left my world. All around me were blackened shades of grey. I lived in a shadow world. The only bright spark in my life was Jordie. But James hauled him off to a monastery, and the shadows returned. 'Tis why I stopped painting."

Arrowsmith had a lump in his throat. His hand stilled, and he pulled her tighter against him.

"Beth, you are breaking my heart," he rasped.

"Now the color is back, Ewan, but I am afraid that if I lose you again, I'll fade to nothing."

Arrowsmith growled and rolled her onto her back, caging her body with his. "Then it is my job to make sure you only see color every day."

"Yes, Ewan, you better make certain of it," Beth grinned, and Arrowsmith set about pleasuring her for the sixth time.

Full Circle

IT WAS NOW SPRING IN the Highlands, and the Arrowsmiths had fully settled into their new home in Scotland. Arrowsmith owned a sizable piece of land and had guardsmen patrolling regularly. He would not take any chances with the safety of his family. His parents lived close by, and they welcomed Beth and Jordie with enthusiasm.

The house was large, and Beth filled it with vibrant color. Her paintings were strewn about the place in organized chaos. There were sketches of Arrowsmith and Jordie, of crofters and neighbors. Ducks, meadows, fields, flowers, and rolling hills. Beth painted her feelings onto the canvas, and Arrowsmith loved what her works portrayed.

Visitors often frequented their house as they were not too far from The MacGregors and the Robertsons when they were in residence. They also had the occasional guests from Northumbria, such as Jean-Luc and Pierre. And so, they slowly began living their dream and building a new life for themselves, creating fresh memories to replace the old.

On one particularly crisp morning, their peace was interrupted when a cart came rumbling up the path. Beth wondered who it could be. Arrowsmith remained cautious of strangers.

They watched from the front window as a man dressed in black alighted the conveyance. He was a nobleman, although he looked slightly disheveled.

When he looked up at the house, Beth paled and gasped in shock.

"Who is that man, Mama?" Jordie asked.

Arrowsmith replied, "'Tis nobody. Son, go see Cook in the kitchen for treats; your mama and I need to speak in private."

Jordie nodded and took off to the kitchen.

Arrowsmith clenched his fists, then stormed out to the front steps.

"You dare show your face here? You need to leave before I kill you," he roared.

Robert Wakefield lifted his palms in peace. "Please, brother, I need to speak to Beth."

"Dinnae call me brother!"

Beth came running out and shouted, "Why, Robert? Why? Go away!"

Arrowsmith held her tight at his side. "You have one minute to leave my property, Robert, before I kill you," he said.

Robert spoke regardless of the rising tension. "Please, I need to make this right; please hear me out. I have Jordan's inheritance."

He held out a bundle of parchments. Beth and Arrowsmith did not move.

"Grandfather is dead. When he died, I found these; it's our inheritance, Beth, which is also Jordan's."

"What do you mean?" Beth asked.

"Speak your piece then get off my land," Arrowsmith growled.

"Grandfather stole from us, Beth. He stole a future from all of us. He told me if you did not marry a nobleman, he would cut me off. I could not afford to be poor, Beth. I owed so many dangerous people money, so I went along with it."

"What is all this?" Arrowsmith asked of the parchments Robert held out.

"'Tis Beth's share of all our assets. It turns out, Grandfather was living on our inheritance. He could not cut us off even if he wanted to because our parents, they left everything to us. He hoped we would never find out, so he had you married off and he pretended to cut me off."

Arrowsmith gritted his teeth and clenched his fists. "That still doesn't explain why you had me attacked."

Robert shook his head. "'Twas not me. Grandfather arranged it all. The missive was fake; he handed it to me, and I believed it too. When I gave it to you, Beth, I thought in honesty Arrowsmith was dead."

Beth looked upset with the revelation. "I did not have to marry at all?"

"No, Beth, we could have hidden you away at the estate forever."

Arrowsmith could see Beth beginning to unravel. So, he pulled her tighter against him and urgently whispered in her ear, "'Tis the past, Beth, it is the past. It canna hurt us now. Dinnae let it take anymore from us."

She nodded.

"Why could you not tell me this before?" Arrowsmith asked.

"Because I was jealous of you, Arrowsmith."

"You were jealous of me?"

"Yes, you had it all, damn you."

"What the devil are you talking about, Robert? I didn't have two sceats to rub together."

"That's the thing, Ewan, you never needed money to get by in the world. I mean, bloody hell, look at you now. Good lord, you work for a blasted king. You never needed a title or riches when greatness is in your blood."

"I canna believe this; we were brothers, you had it all, Robert, everything, and you took Beth away from me!" Arrowsmith roared.

"I had nothing, Ewan! I was broke. My debts crippled us. Beth was my only way out. So, my grandfather fed me a lie, and in desperation, I believed him."

Arrowsmith looked at him with disgust and shook his head.

"You don't understand, Ewan, without a title and wealth, I am nothing! I cannot work with my hands or fight; all I knew was drink and wenching. If it was not for you, I would have died several times over."

"Yet you still betrayed me and Beth."

They were silent a long time. Then Arrowsmith said, "You should have trusted me, Rob. I would have taken care of you both."

"I believe that now. I have nothing to show for my life except regret and a rotten liver," Robert replied, defeated.

Beth stepped forward and took the parchments. She saw her brother for the first time in years, and time had not been kind to him at all. He was a broken man. Then she glanced at her husband and took in her surroundings and realized she had *everything*, and nothing from her past could steal her joy.

"Thank you, Robert. Now I think 'tis best you leave... but, mayhap in the future you could visit when we have had some warning," she said.

Robert's expression softened, and he nodded. "I am truly sorry, Beth, but yes, I would like that."

He turned to Arrowsmith. "I am sorry, Ewan, more than you will ever know."

"So am I, Rob, so am I. It seems we have all been given a second chance to make things right." Arrowsmith sighed, and the tension left him.

Epilogue

1047 - Scotland

B eth felt a presence beside her as gentle fingers brushed against her cheek.

"Beth... love... wake up, our daughter is hungry."

Beth slowly opened her eyes and was greeted with the view of her husband hovering beside the bed, gently rocking their three-month-old baby girl, Clarissa, named after the woman who saved Beth's life and brought them back together.

The babe was whimpering as her father hummed a tune to settle her. Holding her against his bare chest, Arrowsmith whispered in her ear, "Shh sweeting, your ma is coming, love."

Beth's heart melted every time she watched her husband with their children. She smiled and sat up, resting against the headboard. She stretched her arms out as Arrowsmith gently handed Clarissa over for her nightly breastfeeding.

Arrowsmith walked to the other side of the bed where Jordie lay curled up asleep, clutching half-drawn sketches and paintings. He had inherited his mother's artistic eye. Arrowsmith lifted his son into his arms, carried him to the adjoining room, and settled Jordie in his small bed. He bent down and kissed Jordie's forehead, then tucked his blanket around him.

Arrowsmith returned to sit up in bed beside Beth. He was greeted with the contented sound of loud suckling and gulping from his daughter, who was obviously famished. He'd missed out on this with

Jordie, and he was determined not to miss a single moment of his children's lives ever again.

He chuckled as he watched his daughter gorge herself without a care in the world. "I canna believe something so small can eat so much," he said.

Beth just giggled and replied, "She takes after you."

"I dinnae eat a lot," Arrowsmith said in mocked outrage, then leaned across and kissed Beth on the lips.

Their intimate embrace was interrupted by a high-pitched growling sound coming from baby Clarissa, who was annoyed her mother was not focusing on her.

Her parents stared down at their baby girl glaring up at them.

"Now she takes after you!" Arrowsmith said before Beth burst out laughing.

Arrowsmith loved the sound of Beth's laughter. It filled him with joy every time he made her smile. He would kill to keep those smiles coming. He loved these precious moments when it was just him and Beth and their bairns. This was always his dream: to have Beth by his side and a home filled with bairns, love, and laughter. It was not lost on him how close he came to forfeiting his dream. As he reflected, Arrowsmith realized he truly was a blessed man and, for the first time in his life, he knew what it meant to win the ultimate prize.

Sorcha

SORCHA CLIMBED OUT the window of Zala's old cottage and sprinted for the woods. She had never done anything this unexpected or reckless before. For once, she just wanted to go to the village without a troupe of guards trailing behind. She needed some freedom to be a young woman and talk to men without her brothers pummeling them for smiling at her. It was truly shocking how terrified men her age were of Beiste, Brodie, and Dalziel. She still remembered being mortified when Dalziel held one young lad at knifepoint for trying to kiss her when she was younger. Sorcha was extremely put out because that was to be her first kiss until all hell broke loose. After that, the marriageable male population gave her a wide berth. Some even refused to make eye contact with her at the May Day dance because Beiste declared he would banish any man who dared to dance with her.

Her sisters-in-law tried to help her gain more freedom, but it did not work. This was why Sorcha decided at two and twenty years of age she had to take matters into her own hands if she wanted any chance of finding a man to love her.

Fortunately, she had made firm friends with a woman named Tyra who was new to the area. Tyra convinced Sorcha to escape so they could attend the Village Festival together. Tyra lent Sorcha her clan's airisaidh and hair dye to hide her golden locks. She also arranged a meeting point. Tasting freedom for the first time, Sorcha headed out disguised and unrecognizable. She was determined that this year she was going to get her first dance and her very first kiss.

The Battle Cry

SOMETIME LATER, THE doors to the Great Hall at MacGregor Keep burst open as Jordie and the older MacGregor children came in shouting for help. They were hysterical, panicked, and out of breath.

Beiste, Brodie, Dalziel, and Arrowsmith immediately ran towards them, trying to decipher what was happening as they were all talking at once.

It was Amelia who took charge. "Stop! Iona, you speak first, tell us clearly what has happened, right now!" she demanded.

"Mama, a man in the woods took Aunt Sorcha."

Amelia gasped in shock. Clarissa, Zala, and Beth now joined the group.

The men were already gathering their weapons as they fired questions at the children.

"Where exactly and how long ago?" Beiste asked, with his jaw clenched.

"By the rowan tree, there were two men and a lady on horseback," Izara replied.

"'Twas about midday," Colban added.

"We wanted to give chase, but Jordie told us to come for help," Thorfinn piped in.

"Aye, it was good advice, you're all too young to take on grown men," Dalziel said.

The war band was already heading out the door from Beiste's silent command.

"I shot one of them in the thigh with my sharp arrow," Iona added. "He started shouting, and we ran."

"Do you ken who they were?" Brodie asked.

"I ken one man," Jordie replied.

"Who is he, son?" Arrowsmith asked, placing his hand on Jordie's shoulder.

"Da, it was the Highlander who saved me during the snowstorm."

The group was quiet for a moment as they pondered what it could mean.

"The man Iona shot, he called out his name," Colban said.

"What's his name, son?" Beiste asked.

"Bram. He called him Bram," Colban replied.

"Then Bram is a dead man," Beiste said before roaring a battle cry and a call to arms.

The End

Up next Sorcha and Bram's story...

https://elinaemerald.com/[1]

Buy Direct & Save

https://payhip.com/elinaemerald

Sign up for Elina's Newsletter

https://dl.bookfunnel.com/aiq0ubhpx6

Thank you for reading this book. If you enjoyed it, feel free to leave a rating or review.

Elina x

info@elinaemerald.com

---

1. https://elinaemerald.com/books

Also by Elina Emerald

Cambridge
Lucas
Victor: Cambridge Book 2

FRIVEN EMPIRE
The Eleventh House: A Sci-fi Romance
The Vedora Key: A Sci-fi Romance
The Dead of Winter: A Sci-fi Romance

Keeper of Secrets
Highland Warrior: Keeper of Secrets
Highland Guard

Reformed Rogues
Betrothed to the Beast
Betrothed to the Beast
Handfasted to the Bear
Pledged to the Wolf

The MacGregors
Arrowsmith
Sorcha
Lachlan

Standalone
Reformed Rogues plus Arrowsmith Book Bundle
Highlander Undone
His Runaway Bride
To Tame a Viking Warlord

Watch for more at https://elinaemerald.com/books.

www.ingramcontent.com/pod-product-compliance
Lightning Source LLC
Chambersburg PA
CBHW031840170626
46807CB00004B/1550